THE SHORT CREEK RUSTLERS

Neighbours in the Short Creek basin become suspicious of one another when two of their largest cattle operations are victims of cattle rustlers. Elias Fagan, a drifting cowboy, having previously worked with the law, agrees to investigate — covertly. However, someone tries to ambush him before he even reaches Short Creek — and later he's savagely beaten in town. Then, outlaws from the old Hole-in-the-Wall gang turn up and recognise him — it seems there's more than just cattle theft going on . . .

Books by J. D. Ryder
in the Linford Western Library:

SACRED HILLS MASSACRE

J. D. RYDER

THE SHORT CREEK RUSTLERS

Complete and Unabridged

LINFORD
Leicester

First published in Great Britain in 2009 by
Robert Hale Limited
London

First Linford Edition
published 2010
by arrangement with
Robert Hale Limited
London

The moral right of the author has been asserted

British Library CIP Data

Ryder, J. D., *1937 –*
    The Short Creek rustlers. - -
(Linford western library)
1. Western stories.
2. Large type books.
I. Title II. Series
823.9'2–dc22

ISBN 978–1–44480–325–9

Published by
F. A. Thorpe (Publishing)
Anstey, Leicestershire

Set by Words & Graphics Ltd.
Anstey, Leicestershire
Printed and bound in Great Britain by
T. J. International Ltd., Padstow, Cornwall

This book is printed on acid-free paper

1

George Crauley Junior knew he was going to have trouble explaining to his pa what had happened, but he'd have to do it. There weren't no way around it. The fella was following him, wasn't he? What else could he do but shoot him?

Junior had been surprised when he saw who the rider coming up the road behind him was. It was hard to figure. There the fella was, sitting so high and mighty in the saddle, loping along like he was going to a picnic. Probably didn't think anyone would know he was a lawman. But Junior had seen him down there by the loading pens, there in Golden, hadn't he? Yes, sir. Sure enough, standing there talking to that federal marshal just like they was planning something. Pa would certainly want to know about this jasper, yes sir.

It'd been lucky he had stopped on

that little rise to study his back trail. Pa thought he didn't have enough brains but everybody knew you had to be careful. Especially when you was carrying cash money. That's when he'd seen that rider.

Too far away to see who it was, but shucks, there'd only be one thing an outsider would find interesting in coming up to the basin. That'd be cattle. Wouldn't likely be his pa's horse ranch. No, it'd be cattle. That's what folks are talking about, ain't it? Rustlers? Yeah, maybe he'd better hang back and see if he could find out something about this galloot.

It was a good thing he did, too. Reining his sorrel off the road he'd been lucky to find a place in the shade of a big oak tree where he'd be out of sight and could still see what was what. Standing there, he watched as the rider came along, resting like in the saddle.

The horse he was riding was a light brown-dun mustang. Probably had some mixed blood, Junior thought, seeing what looked like zebra striping on the animal's legs. A fine animal for cattle work, mustangs were. Since moving in on that ranch Pa had been dealing with mustangs a lot, selling them to the surrounding ranches. But it was the Arabian breed that was the money animal. Those, Junior knew, he didn't often sell. Usually Pa would take one in trade from some fella or another that come riding in on a weary, saddle sore horse and ride out on one of pa's Arabs. Pa'd bring that horse back to good health and sooner or later trade it off too. Usual there was some money made in the trading.

That was the one rule of Pa's you didn't buck. You never talked about those horses or the men that rode in, usually in the dark of night to trade. Say something about those men and you'd get a whipping. That's why Pa'd want to know about this jasper riding by. He was somehow connected to that federal marshal and Pa wouldn't like having him coming into the basin, no sir.

Junior smiled as he thought about how proud Pa'd be if he stopped the lawman from getting any closer to Short Creek and the B-slash-B. Pa was always saying how Junior didn't have anything under his hat but hair. Well, this'd prove different.

He hadn't thought much about it but was darn glad he'd brought his Winchester off the saddle. Leaning against the rough bark of the tree, Junior sighted down the barrel and squeezed the trigger.

Blinded by the flash, he didn't see exactly what happened, but after blinking a bit, his eyes cleared and he could see the mustang running on down the road, the saddle empty and the stirrups flapping. Junior had done good, he'd shot the fella right outa the saddle.

Cranking another shell into the breech, he strode out on to the road expecting to see the man's body. It'd likely be a good thing, he thought, to drag it back into the trees. Coyotes and other scavengers would take care of it.

There was no sign of the dead lawman.

Quickly searching both sides and down to the river bank, Junior couldn't find anything. Pa wouldn't like that. It wasn't gonna be easy trying to tell him about it, either.

★   ★   ★

Fagan hadn't been dozing in the saddle, he'd just been resting. When the mustang's ears twitched and had ducked his head to look toward the trees, the rider had moved instinctively, falling out of the saddle on the other side. The scream of the bullet passing by his head was loud in his ear. The man's sudden movement had frightened the dun-colored horse, sending it in panic down the road.

Holding tightly to the Henry he'd pulled from the scabbard, Fagan let his body roll away and into a stand of willows. Lying still for a moment he thought about what had happened. He wasn't exactly sure where the shooter had been hidden and wasn't sure how well hidden he was. Crouching down and keeping his gaze on the trees, he started to move stealthily further back into the brush. Stepping back, the ground suddenly gave way under his feet and he fell backward, landing with a splash in the fast-moving river.

★ ★ ★

Fagan had been watching the river since the road swung close to it. Maybe, after finding out what he could about what was happening in Short Creek, he'd take time to do some fishing. From what he could see, the river was a series of fast-flowing rapids and then a stretch of quiet, calm only to be followed by more white water. There just had to be trout in there.

It was near the end of one set of

rapids that he fell into. Hitting the water, he was washed downstream, unable to stop being knocked about. Finally sinking into a deep hole, and still gripping his rifle in one hand, he surged to the surface gasping for air. Eyes wide with panic, he spotted the root of a tree as big as his arm inches in front of his face. Grabbing the solid brace he fought to keep his head up. Elias Christian Fagan had never learned how to swim.

Catching his breath, he shook the water out of his ears before pulling himself up on to solid ground. Water squished in his boots as he moved up the river bank. Someone had tried to kill him, he couldn't forget that.

A clump of tall, whip-like willows grew next to the road, giving him enough cover. Leaning forward he looked up the road and watched as a man, leading a horse by the reins stepped out of the trees. Standing in the shadows, the man took a long look around before swinging into the saddle and, poking a boot heel into the horse's side, rode out of sight. All Fagan could tell was the man who had tried to ambush him had been big and broad shouldered.

2

The mustang was calmly chomping grass off to the side of the wagon road about a mile from where the shooting had taken place. Fagan had worried about that, hoping the shooter hadn't simply taken the horse. It was still a long way into Short Creek.

Off the road a piece, he found a likely spot and, after hanging his soggy clothes in the afternoon sun, he started a small cook fire. Heating water he dropped the last of his coffee beans into the fire-blackened coffee pot and sat back to work on his rifle and belt-gun and to think things out.

Nobody was to know the reason for him going up to Short Creek and had anyone heard about it, it was unlikely they could get that far ahead of him. He and Marshal Frank Goodall had finished their talk only that morning and no one had passed him on the road. Something else was going on and somehow he'd got into the middle of it.

Well, he thought as he poured the strong-smelling brew into a tin cup, whatever it could be had nothing to do with him. Settling back, he watched as dusk came on, enjoying the quiet of the forest around him and the last of his hot coffee. Tomorrow he'd be in Short Creek. There would likely be a few days, maybe even a week or so, before any more trouble would come his way. He'd have that time to relax and enjoy small-town life before his work got in the way.

Riding into town sometime after noon he decided the first thing to do would be to replenish his empty saddle-bags and then have a drink; he certainly wasn't looking for trouble. Somehow trouble found him, though, before he'd been in town ten minutes.

The tall lanky rider wasn't exactly sure what he was riding into, but after agreeing to help out when the federal marshal asked for a favor he figured it'd be best to take things slow and easy. At least until he found out what he was up against. From what little he'd been told, there wasn't a real hurry so the young cowboy was, as his pa would say, 'just moseying along.'

Dropping the reins of his dun over the hitch rail in front of the building marked SALOON, he slowly unwound his long-limbed body from the hard-used saddle. Anyone looking his way would know he was a cowboy. Standing better than six feet in his stocking feet, his broad shoulders and thin waist could have described many men in their early twenties. It was the slightly bowed legs encased in thin leather pants, worn shiny where he sat the saddle, high-heeled, pointed-toed riding boots and floppy Stetson that advertised his calling. All that and the holstered Colt belted around his narrow waist.

Stretching tired muscles, he settled the gun-belt, cuffed back his wide-brimmed hat and licked his full lips at the thought of the dust-cutting drink waiting inside. Promising himself a drink after taking care of business at the general store, he untied his saddle-bags and walked across the dirt street.

A four-wheel buggy with a well-matched team of bays stood next to the plank sidewalk in front of the general store. The wagon box and shiny canvas top looked to have been recently painted and looked, he thought, a little out of place in this rural backwater town.

Passing around behind the vehicle, he stepped up on the porch and pushed open the door into the store. The buzz of conversation that he had faintly heard stopped abruptly. Standing a moment to let his eyes adjust from the afternoon sunshine, he smiled at the man and woman standing at the counter watching him.

The man was obviously some kind of dude, Fagan surmised. Growing up as he did in the border country of south Texas, he'd seen a lot of rich Mexicans dressing themselves like a 'Spanish grandee' in silver-studded leather riding gear, usually tight-legged pants that flared out over their high-heeled boots and topped by a short vest covering a brightly colored shirt. Often, these shirts would be ruffled. This man's was and his pants were tight as any Mexican would have worn, but he didn't have the slender body that a caballero had. This fellow was heavily built, a roll of what his ma called 'table muscle' sat easily above his wide leather belt. After his quick glance, Fagan decided it wouldn't be polite to give the man any closer inspection.

Letting his eyes drift to the young woman behind the counter, he instantly looked away. She was too beautiful and if he hadn't been quick he might have ended up staring, which would be unacceptable behavior.

'Howdy,' Fagan mumbled and letting his gaze take in the store. Pulling the saddle-bags off his shoulder and unbuckling them, he smiled. 'Nothing worse than running out of coffee and canned peaches, is there? Coffee, peaches and about everything else,' he said, walking over to a set of shelves and picking up a couple cans. After reading the labels, he dropped them in the bags and, noticing that the couple didn't continue their conversation, decided to ignore them.

★　★　★

Without looking back, he felt the pair watch as he slowly choose his supplies, making his way down one aisle and around the long room, coming back to the counter with the saddle-bags heavily loaded. Keeping his face empty and being careful not to let his eyes linger, he nodded to the woman.

'Ma'am, how about cutting off a piece of that rat cheese,' he said, holding his fingers apart to measure. She wasn't much more than a girl, he saw, a very pretty girl. Fagan let his smile grow. Her head was covered with

14

long blonde hair that hung to her shoulders, ending with a soft curl. The hair was held back from her ears by mother-of-pearl clips, framing her face. High cheekbones were a rosy color on either side of her long, but not too long, thin, but not too thin, nose. Her blue eyes fell down to the wheel of yellow cheese when she caught him studying her. Fagan tried not to stare, but something about looking at her made him feel good.

'Harrumph', the man who had been standing on the customer side of the counter cleared his throat. 'A gentleman shouldn't stare at a lady,' his words were clipped and for an instant, Fagan thought he was somehow talking through his nose.

Glancing at the man, the cowboy smiled. 'You are right, of course. But like a beautiful sunset or the first rose of spring, when a man sees a very beautiful woman he must not pass up the opportunity to pay full homage.'

'Oh, you're making me blush,' the

young woman said, her words soft and light.

'Say, there — ' The man started to speak but was cut off when the girl, ignoring him, spoke to Fagan.

'You are new to Short Creek, aren't you?' she asked, 'I don't think I've ever seen you before.'

'You called it, ma'am. Just rode in a few minutes ago,' hearing the man shuffling his feet, he decided to tease. 'I was figuring on riding on. Well, maybe stay a night or two, get a hotel bed for a change, before heading on north. But now, well, might be worth it to stop and look around a little.' He let his smile grow, 'you know, see what this country has to offer.'

'There isn't anything here that would be worth a drifter's time,' the man spoke up, his accent very pronounced.

'You think I'm just a drifting cowhand?' Fagan glanced at him and laughed as he buckled up his saddle-bags. 'Why everyone knows you can't tell a horse by its color. I may look a

16

little rough around the edges, but that's 'cause I've been riding. No, I'm actually the scion of a huge cattle ranch down in Texas.'

'Harrumph,' the man snorted again. 'That is, without a doubt, the biggest lie I've ever heard.'

Fagan stopped moving and let his smile fall away.

'Mister, I don't know who you are and I don't know where you come from, but calling a man a liar is dangerous talk. I don't see that you're packing a six-gun so I'll just chalk it up to ignorance, but was you to go using those words again, you'd better be finding a weapon mighty fast.'

'Boys,' the young woman broke in, 'there will be no more of that kind of talk. Winston, you are out of line; this man is right. I don't want to hear anymore of that, not in my store or around me. Do you hear?'

The two men stood staring at each other for a long moment before Winston let his body relax.

'Of course. How boorish of me. Sir,' he said formerly, giving Fagan a slight bow, 'I apologize.' Turning to the girl he tipped his hat, 'Miss Duniway, I apologize to you also. It will not happen again. Now, if you'll forgive me, I must return to the, uh, ranch.'

Turning without giving Fagan any further notice, his back held straight and stiff, he strode out of the store.

'I'm sorry, mister,' the woman said softly. 'Winston is not from here. I mean he is a local in that he, or his family, owns Crown, the biggest ranch in the basin. But he was raised in the east, in New York so he doesn't know, sometimes, how things here are done.'

'Easterner, huh. I caught his accent. It's pretty classy, I'll say.' Giving her his biggest smile, he continued with his flirting, 'Now, I've found out you are single, your name is Duniway and you own this store. What else can you tell me about yourself? What's your front name?'

Blushing and looking down at her

hands, she was still for a bit before looking up. 'Abigail Duniway is my name, although my friends call me Abby. You may call me Miss Duniway. My father, Clarence Duniway, owns the store and if you have thoughts about me, you might as well keep riding. Winston has asked me to marry him.' She hesitated, and then went on. 'Well, he hasn't exactly proposed yet, but we have talked about getting married and I know he will. So you can just keep riding. That'll be five dollars, please.'

Chuckling at the seriousness of her voice, Fagan reached into a pocket and brought out a few coins. 'Five dollars and well worth it, Miss Duniway, well worth it.'

Throwing the saddle-bags over his shoulder and still laughing, he walked to the front of the store. Stopping with one hand on the door, he turned back and laughing again, walked out.

★ ★ ★

The smile on his face was huge as he tied the saddle-bags on behind the cantle. All laughter disappeared when someone grabbed his arms. Instantly twisting, he fought but stopped when he found he was being firmly held by two strong men.

'What the hell — ' He started to yell then stopped when he looked up to find the Easterner standing in front of him.

'I didn't appreciate your little scene in front of Miss Duniway, drifter,' Winston said coldly, pulling on a pair of thin leather riding gloves. 'One must be taught not to talk to a lady in such a manner. Men, if you'd be so kind as to keep him secure?' Not waiting for a response, he buried his gloved fist deep in Fagan's belly.

The lanky cowboy fought to breathe, trying to inhale. Unable to do more than gulp air, he stood helpless, half hanging from the hold the two men had on his upper arms. The roar in his ears grew when he was struck again, this time the leather gloved fist slamming

Fagan's bowed head, splitting the skin above his eyebrow. Blood spurted and for a second the Easterner just stood motionless, before curling his lips and smashing the wounded man in the ribs.

Again and again Fagan's stomach was pummelled until, still not given a chance to fill his lungs, the two men gripping his arms let him crumble to the ground.

'Damn it, men,' Winston growled, 'hold him up.'

'Naw, boss, he's done.'

Gasping for air, Fagan didn't have the strength to move, even to protect his head when a handful of hair was grabbed and his face lifted out of the dirt.

'Now listen to me, you drifting scum. Ride on. There is nothing in this town or in the basin for you. You have purchased your supplies so there is no reason for you to return to the market. Get on your sorry-looking beast and don't stop anywhere close to here.' Letting go, he let Fagan's face fall. The cowboy had passed out and didn't feel it.

3

'Come on, mister; let's get you out of the street.' Fagan felt himself picked up bodily and held until he was able to get his feet under him. Taking a deep breath, he winced from a sharp pain in his side.

'Ah, well now, Bucko,' the deep rumble of words seemed to flow over Fagan's ears like soft, pillowing cotton. 'Let me get a shoulder under your arm. Easy now, take it some easy. From the moaning and groaning, I'd guess you've got a busted rib or two. Come on, now.'

Leaning against the man who had picked him up, Fagan focused on making his legs move and at the same time fighting to fill his lungs.

'Thanks,' he said, trying not to whimper.

Sounding as if coming from a deep

well, the man half-carrying him chuckled. 'It was a harsh beating you were given and that's for sure. And I've seen a few in my time, I have. We'll get old Doc Adams to fix that cut over your eye and tape you up tight and in a few days you'll be near back to feeling alive.'

'The welcome given to a man coming into your little town is worth bragging about,' Fagan's voice sounded weak to his ears. 'The fella that worked me over, did you see who it was?'

'Ach, yes and I saw the whole blamed thing. When those two ruffians took aholt of you, I stopped me work. By the time I got my eyes cleared the cowhands was hooked on and that big foreigner was busy cleaning your plow. I come arunning but by that time they was through making their point and was walking away.'

Letting the cowboy stand leaning over with his head hanging, resting, he introduced himself. 'I'm Eloy Marchal, by the way. Working over yonder as the blacksmith. Been a lot of things, as most folk are, and right now I'm the man who puts shoes on the town's horses.'

Fagan shook his head, still breathing deeply. 'Appreciate your help, Mr Marchal.' Looking up at the other man, he asked, his voice still sounding thin and weak. 'Is this the town's typical welcome to strangers?'

The burly man laughed. 'Nope, it isn't. But you seemed to get on the wrong side of our local example of royalty.'

Watchful of how he moved, Fagan nodded. 'Yeah, it was some kind of greenhorn that did this. Some dude going by the name of Winston.'

'Yup, Winston Moncrieffe Peeters is the full name. P-E-E-T-E-R-S,' Marchal spelled it out as they walked. 'Story goes he's a remittance man, sent out here to the wild west so as to get his self taught how to be a man. Doesn't appear to be working, though. Here, step up on the porch and we'll see if Doc Adams is anywhere near sober enough to fix you up.'

Careful not to cause the beaten man any unnecessary pain, the doctor helped him remove his shirt. Standing back, he slowly walked around Fagan, mumbling to himself about the bruising that was starting to show. Rolling up the sleeves of his shirt, he motioned for Fagan to sit down on a backless high stool.

Muttering to himself he carefully washed the drying blood from the man's face.

'That cut looked a lot worse than it really is,' said the doctor. 'I don't think I'll need to sew it up.' Taking care, he closed the cut and held the edges together with a strip of sticky tape.

'Looks like you got too close to the back leg of a mule,' Adams murmured, crouching to peer at Fagan's chest, 'and let him kick you over and over.'

Muttering to himself, he gently poked and prodded. Fagan quietly took the inspection until a finger touched a sore place on his side.

'Hey, easy there, Doc. No reason for you to make it any worse than it is.'

'Yes, there's a broken rib or two in there. But,' he gently ran a finger along the bones, feeling his way, 'it isn't as bad as it could have been. Umm, yes, I'll tape it up good and tight, give the bone some support and it'll heal up in no time. The bruising'll last a lot longer though.'

'Ya see, Bucko, ain't that just about what I told ya?'

'Eloy Marchal,' Doc Adams said severely, 'you tend to your forge and horseshoes and leave the doctoring to me.'

While Adams started wrapping wide tape around Fagan's chest, the cowboy looked over at the burly man.

'So, you're the village blacksmith? I must make sure you get all my work from here on out. Least I can do for picking me up and bringing me here. Thank you,' he said, holding out his hand. 'My name's Fagan, Elias Christian Fagan, if you have to have the full handle, but I answer quicker to just Fagan.'

While the doctor worked on his body Fagan looked the blacksmith over and decided Eloy Marchal was built like most smithys he'd known. Stockily built with a mane of black hair falling over his ears, the man was dressed in bib overalls, the suspender straps laying flat over his broad heavily muscled shoulders. If this was the blacksmith, where was his thick leather apron?

'There,' Doc Adams said, finishing a double layer of wide sticky tape around his body, 'that'll do ya. Now I gotta warn ya not to go getting into any more fights, at least not for a few weeks. Let those bones heal up.'

Marchal chuckled again. 'No, Doc, that wasn't no fight this bucko was in. No sir, it was as good a beatin' as I ever saw.'

Doc Adams smiled as he rolled his shirt sleeves down. 'Well, that's all right by me. Most of my medicating comes

27

from fixing up men who got beat up or shot. Talking about my fee, if you got the money, cowboy, it'll be two dollars for the tape and a drink over at the saloon for me putting it around you.'

Digging into a pants pocket, Fagan dropped a couple coins into the doctor's palm. 'Now a drink sounds good to me. That was next on my list of things to do, after stopping at the general store. Mr Marchal, would you join us and let me start to repay you for your help and assistance?'

The smithy nodded and after helping Fagan get his shirt on, held the door for the other men to walk out.

'Tell me the truth,' Fagan said as the three men walked down the street, 'does that easterner take dislike to every man who says howdy to that pretty girl over in the general store?'

'Nope,' Marchal shook his head. 'Our tenderfoot is pretty well appreciated in Short Creek, and when he decided it was our store-owner's daughter he was going to marry, it didn't take much for everyone to know to walk and talk gently around her. You musta flirted a little too much when you was getting your supplies.'

'You say he's well liked here; is that because of his wedding plans?'

'Nope, it's because his family owns the most prosperous spread in this part of the state. It's certainly the largest outfit. Not counting the open range the Crown ranch runs cattle on and you're talking, what'd you say, Doc, a hundred thousand acres they filed on? Why, just look at the number of riders out there and you can see where this town's bread gets its butter.'

'Where you call home, cowboy?' Doc Adams cut in.

'Oh, down Texas way,' said Fagan. 'Pa's got a cattle outfit down there along the border. But you know how it is, there's a lot of world to see so I went to ride out to take a look.'

★ ★ ★

Junior was too big for his pa to whip him any more, but that didn't mean he got off easy when he tried to explain what had happened.

'Damn it, boy, all you was to do was take that string of mares down and meet up with the buyer and bring the money back. That's all. Nobody said anything about dry-gulching some ranny you saw talking with that badge-toting lawman. You better hope nobody sees the body and recognizes the fella, is all I can say.'

Junior shook his head and kept his eyes on the floor, afraid the old man would read that something was wrong. It'd only make it worse to admit he hadn't found the body. Hell, at that range he couldn't have missed, could he?

It was a work day, but the Crauleys had taken up space at the far end of the bar. A couple B-slash-B riders had ridden in with the horse breeder, were leaning against the mahogany a few steps away and hadn't heard the two

30

talking. The elder Crauley had just finished berating his son when Junior let out a gasp.

Looking over his pa's shoulder, Junior was idly watching the door and when he saw who was coming right behind the blacksmith and the town doctor, he nearly fainted. Grabbing his pa's arm, he shuddered.

'What the hell?' George Crauley snarled, then seeing the look on Junior's face stopped. Looking to see what had scared the boy, he frowned.

'What's the matter, Junior?' Crauley whispered coarsely.

'That's him, Pa. That's the man I . . . oh, gawd, that's the man on the trail.'

'Hey,' said one of the men standing next to George Crauley, 'I know that dude from somewhere. Yeah, his mug is . . . I've seen him before.'

'From where, Russell?' Crauley snarled. 'Who the hell is he?'

'I don't know right off. But there's something about him that's familiar.'

'Well, think on it and let me know.

Now, Junior,' he turned back to his son and, keeping his voice low, gave his order, 'shut up and keep your eye on the fella.'

* * *

Talk ceased when the three men stepped up and pushed through the swinging bat-wing doors.

Inside, the big blacksmith and the doctor didn't hesitate but stepped over to the mahogany bar. Fagan stopped just inside the door to let his eyes adjust to the dimness of the room. Slowly looking around, he saw he was the center of attention. Well, he smiled to himself, that's typical of a small town. Everyone wants to check out the stranger. Nodding to the room in general, he stepped over to join the others.

'Whiskey, if it comes out of a bottle, beer if not,' he let his smile soften his words.

The bartender, a short stocky man

wearing a round-topped derby and standing about halfway along the back bar, frowned at him before, taking his time, he began to slowly fill a beer mug. Fagan frowned and glanced to the men standing on the other side of the polished bar and found more unfriendly faces.

Junior was sure he was done for, but when the newcomer didn't seem to recognize him, he wondered.

'Hey, Pa,' the boy whispered, 'maybe he didn't see me after all. If'n he had, he'd be coming for me, wouldn't he?'

George Crauley stood for a moment then smiled evilly. 'Yeah, I reckon,' he mumbled. Then taking a close look at Fagan, he frowned. 'Hey, that's the fella that got beat up out in the street. Call him out, Junior. That's one sure way to tell if he knows ya.'

'Ah, Pa, what if he does?'

'In that case ya got me here to cover ya. Go on now, do what you're told.'

Junior hesitated and then, more afraid of his pa than the stranger, he stepped away from the bar. 'Who the hell are you?' he snarled as meanly as he could.

'What the hell do you care?' Fagan snapped back angrily. Getting shot at and then beaten up for no reason he could see was all he was going to take. He'd had enough grief and wasn't going to take any more.

Putting down his beer glass, Fagan was about to turn when Marchal held up a big scarred hand. 'Now back off, Junior. This man has been injured and Doc Adams has prescribed whiskey as the right medicine.'

The man asking the question had stepped away from the small crowd down the bar and stood facing him. 'We saw what kind of injuries he's got,' the man barked. 'Mr Peeters wouldn't go beating on anyone less'n he had a good enough reason. Now you come bringing him in here and we want to know what it was all about.'

Fagan turned and, taking a step away from the bar, stood taking his time, looked the man up and down. A paid thug, he decided, noting that the fella was built like a water tank, thick-muscled shoulders sitting on top of a barrel of a chest. The man's black hair had been cropped close to his square-shaped head leaving only an inch or so of forehead above a single black eyebrow protecting a pair of eyes that were deep-set black marbles. Young, tough and sure of himself, more than likely a bully, Fagan thought, and was about to say something when the thug, his body tensing, went on.

'Ain't anyone welcome in here that's gonna cause trouble for Crown. Now, I'll ask again politely, who the hell are ya?'

Slowly shaking his head and just as slow reaching his left hand up to push back his hat, Fagan let his right hand drop to rest on the butt of his Colt. Thumbing the thong off the exposed hammer, he let a humorless smile twist his lips.

'My ma taught me good manners,

especially when talking to strangers. Seems yore ma, if'n you had one, missed giving you that class.'

'What the — ?' the tough started, taking a step forward only to be halted by the man standing beside him. His words were filled with authority.

'That's enough, Junior. The man is right, he's a guest in our little town and he'll be treated as such. Leastways until we find out if he's a troublemaker or not.'

For a long moment, the rowdy lout stood tense, before shrugging, he stepped back. Fagan kept his eyes on him for another moment and then totally ignoring the young bully, turned his head to look at the one giving the orders.

'Thanks,' he said, keeping his voice soft. 'It appears you might have saved me from having to hurt someone.'

'Dammit — ' Junior started again only to be stopped when the boss called his name.

'That'll be enough.' His voice cut like

a whip. Waiting a long minute, the man looked back at Fagan and smiled. Fagan noticed the smile didn't soften his eyes any. 'You might or might not hurt the boy, but what about the rest of my men?'

'Oh, I reckon I'd have to hurt a few of them, too, if they wanted to get involved.'

The man laughed coldly and moving slowly, stood up to stand next to the one called Junior with his hands on his hips. He was an older version of the tough. More wrinkles in the skin of his face and salt and pepper gray hair instead of coal black hair. But close enough to be clear this was the father.

'I like a man with spirit, I surely do.' Putting his hand out, he smiled and took the few steps toward Fagan. 'I'm George Crauley, and that young man you just called a bastard is my son, George Jr. My wife, his mother, died a while back.'

Fagan made a show of grimacing. 'Well, then, I suppose I'd better apologize to young George's father. Maybe when the lesson was handed out, the youngster was merely off somewhere playing.'

Crauley laughed out loud, at the same time motioning to the bartender.

'Let me buy this man a drink, Otto. Pour them for old Doc Adams and our town's blacksmith while you're at it.' Still with a cold smile plastered on his face, he turned back to Fagan. 'Yes, sir, I do take your point. However,' he stopped as the bartender poured the drinks. Both men picking up their glasses saluted each other and tossed them back.

'Ah, now that does do it right,' Crauley said, nodding at Otto. 'As I was about to say, there are good reasons for my son's unwelcoming demeanor.' Fagan noticed the cold smile was gone. 'The basin needs to keep on the good side of young Mister Peeters, so as one of the smaller ranchers here I do have an interest. What was the fight all about?'

Fagan slowly looked the rancher over then let his eyes take in the rest of the room. Glancing at the bartender he saw that man's hands were out of sight under the bar. Probably got a short-barreled scattergun back there, the cowboy thought, or more likely a short billy club. Looking past Otto he saw the mirrors on the back wall were all blurry and smoke stained. Smiling, he picked up his whiskey and sipped the liquid. Putting it back down, he looked sideways to find Crauley waiting for an answer.

'Nope, I don't think it's any of your business.' Fagan said, keeping his words soft and clear. 'I've been pushed around enough for one day. Now, if'n you want to let your wolf loose, go for it, but know when the ball opens your family is going to come up short a couple members.'

4

Crauley's face blanched and for a long moment nobody spoke.

'Hey, Fagan, let's not forget your busted rib,' Marchal cut in.

'Wait a minute,' one of the Crauley hands said loudly. 'He called you Fagan. You wouldn't be that gunman what they say stopped the Hole-In-The-Wall gang up north, now, would you?'

Fagan smiled humorlessly. 'Well, I was up in Wyoming when a few would-be bad men tried to hold up a bank. Yeah, I guess the newspapers called them a gang but they weren't. Not really. Just a few fools looking to get paid with other people's money.'

'Yeah,' another man standing farther back said, 'and a fast gun going by the name of Fagan up and killed Black Jack Ketchum and Eli Lay. Them two was the worst of the gang. No, sir, Mister Crauley, I'll work your horses for you but if you go pushing this man into a fight, I'll draw my pay first, you don't mind.'

Without looking around Fagan could feel everyone take a mental step back. There wouldn't be any more trouble here. Right now, at least.

'I still don't understand,' Crauley said, 'but I guess it isn't any of my business. C'mon Junior, you've had enough to drink. Let's get back to the ranch.' Not waiting to see if he was followed, the rancher turned and stalked out of the saloon. Soon the only customers left were Fagan and his two new friends.

Outside on the boardwalk, the man named Russell grabbed George Crauley's arm and pulled him aside.

'Yeah, that's Elias Fagan all right. I should have recognized him first off but I didn't. Boss, be careful. He's a tough hombre. Gets his' teeth in something and don't let go. I knew him up in

41

Wyoming, before he took out Jack Ketchum. That day he busted up the gang I was back in the Hole-In-The-Wall. Black Jack didn't know me so good and wouldn't let me ride with him. Damn good thing it was, too. I'd run into Fagan a few days before, when I first rode into Jackson County. He was pointed out to me by Flat Nose Curry. You remember Flat Nose, don't ya?'

'Yeah. Me and him . . . well, never mind. So, this Fagan was toting a badge up in Wyoming and now he's down here. Wonder why?'

Standing with his hands on his hips, he looked sightlessly at the mounted men sitting their saddles waiting for him, lost in thought. Finally, with a shake of his head, he nodded. 'All right, I'll keep Junior on him. Let's get back to the ranch. I expect Nixon to be sending over another little jag of beeves later tonight. C'mon, let's ride.'

★   ★   ★

'Boy, I've been in towns where the augers had control of things, but not like this,' Fagan said, motioning to the bartender for another drink. 'I'll have another beer, Otto, if you don't mind.'

Doc Adams shook his head slowly side to side. Glancing up to find the bartender standing close by wiping a shot glass, he frowned. 'C'mon, let's get a table and be comfortable.'

Pulling chairs from a round table on the far side of the room, the three men sat back.

'To my thinking there's too many of the local businessmen who are a mite quick to bow and scrape to the Crown gang,' the medical man said, nodding back toward the bar. 'Otto is one of the worse, in my view.'

Marchal nodded his agreement. 'Yeah, but Crown is most of the town's business, no question. Of course that shouldn't mean they can run all over everyone or get away with beating up every stranger that comes riding through.'

Fagan smiled and sipped his beer. 'Well, I guess I did make him look a bit bad in front of the beautiful shop-keeper.'

'But to have you held down while he beats on you? That ain't right, even if it did bring some business to my door.'

'No, Doc, it doesn't set right with me, either,' Fagan said. 'Maybe I'll stick around for while. Make riding a lot easier if my ribs are all healed up.'

Marchal shook his head. 'Well, don't go thinking about getting revenge. Young Peeters is never alone. If there ain't a couple hands riding along side there's that foreman, Nixon. He's a real curly wolf and he's got himself a crew of hard cases just like him that hang close by. Better you cut your losses and ride on.'

Fagan emptied his glass and leaned back. 'Well, not for a few days anyway. Think I'll get myself a few nights sleep in a real bed. Maybe enjoy a meal or three that I don't have to cook over a campfire. Uh huh,' he nodded, 'I think that's what the doctor should order.'

The three sat quietly for a time, staring into their empty glasses.

'Are those the only ranchers in this basin?' Fagan asked finally, trying to get the conversation flowing. 'Crown and the one that Crauley runs, is that all?'

'No, there're a few others. None as big as Crown, though. Only other one worth mentioning is Turnbull's Box M. Old man Turnbull's place is up at the head of the basin. It's a likely spread, covers maybe two sections of land. Short Creek, from where it flows out of the badlands over to the west is the border between the Box M and B-slash-B land, south of the creek. The Crauley place is bordered by the badlands on one side and the river on the other. It's not anywhere as big as the Box M, probably about half the size. And then south of there, a bunch of farmers have taken land along the river below him. On the other side of the river all along there is Crown. The river is that spread's western boundary.

Nobody knows exactly where Crown's southern border is. They run cattle on another couple thousand acres of public land further on down, I hear.'

'That makes Crown king of the mountain, then, as far as the town is concerned.'

Marchal slowly nodded his head. 'Well, really all that matters, anyhow. They got the most men and spend the most money here.'

Fagan let the talk die out for a bit then looked up with his next question. 'I just rode up from Golden. Seem to recall hearing some talk down there about ranches up in this part of the country being hit by a plague of rustlers.'

The blacksmith glanced over at the doctor before nodding again. 'Well, yeah. Both Turnbull and Nixon have been complaining about it. Nixon's the Crown foreman. There weren't much said until old man Turnbull got to worrying about losing some young stuff. That opened the gate, you might say. That's about when Nixon allowed they'd probably lost some too. Made some folk wonder what had taken him so long to bring it up. Like maybe he had known about it but didn't want to make people know he knew.'

'Be careful, Eloy,' Doc Adams warned, looking around to make sure nobody was listening. 'Nixon's not likely to allow any talk like that stand.'

'Oh, hell, Doc, you know it yourself. I ain't saying anything everybody else is saying.'

Fagan stepped right in, bringing the conversation back to safer ground. 'So there are only the two big outfits and the horse ranch?'

'Well, yeah, I guess,' Marchal said slowly. 'Course the Box M ain't what you'd call a big spread. Turnbull's got some fine stock though, mostly long-horn and Durham mix. He'll ship maybe a thousand head a year where Crown drives thousands.'

Doc Adams chuckled. 'Of course, there's always the badlands. That's our local answer to anything that goes missing, someone from the badlands took it.'

'What are the badlands?'

Adams shook his head. 'You know how it is, any time you find something folks don't know about there'll be rumors of evil about it. Here it is what everyone calls the badlands. We had a preacher come through one time. Said he'd ridden across that strip of country and nearly died. According to him, it's the remains of an old lava flow, all molten rock that cooled leaving a wide rugged scar on the earth. A land that God left to remind us of His power, the preacher said.'

'I've seen land like that, down south,' said Fagan. 'But usually it turns out to have pockets of good land, trees and such, hidden away.'

'Yeah,' Marchal agreed. 'That's more likely in this case. After all, that's where Short Creek comes out of.'

'But nobody goes in there,' Adams argued. 'It's too barren. I doubt if that has anything to do with the rustling. Any rustled stock is more likely to be driven north, up through the pass over the Moguls.'

'Doc, you just don't know anything about driving cattle. Ain't no cattle gonna be herded up an' over that mountain pass. It's too steep. And where you gonna take them once you get to the other side? Nothing but sand and sagebrush for the next twenty miles or more and no water at all, not until you get clean across that stretch anyhow. Cows gotta have water.'

Fagan smiled, understanding these two men liked to disagree with each other. Once again he changed the subject. 'It looked to me like that Crauley sees himself as being tough.'

'Yeah, both father and son,' said the blacksmith. 'They may be mean spirited and like to bully everybody, but ya gotta give them credit, they do raise good riding stock. They turn out fine riding stock alongside a tolerable supply of working horses. Mostly mustangs, they are, and there ain't no better breed of horse than that for working cattle.'

'Now,' Doc Adams cut in, 'you take a look at that matched pair he sold to Peeters. They are real fine horse flesh. He's getting a reputation for having some of the best Arab stock in the territory. Came into the basin only a year or two back and moved into the old Calhoun place. It'd been empty for years. Story goes that he came out west from somewhere back east, or maybe from one of them southern states. Looked around and the next thing had a herd of horses to sell. Put in a few fences and said he was gonna start breeding horses. Up on the flats, between the river and the bluff, clear back to the edge of the badlands, he's got a bunch of mustangs too. Says he's making pretty good money shipping his better stock east. Mustangs might be the ticket for riding out on the range, but there's a good market for his better stock, too.'

Marschal nodded. 'Yeah, no doubt about it. Crauley and his boys work hard and look to have fast-growing herds. Some surprising, when you think about it. Hells bells, it wasn't so many years ago this was all Indian country. About the same as with Turnbull. He came in and saw that bit of land that Crown didn't have. The Box M had been vacant for a time, the owner and his wife died and the place went fallow. Turnbull showed up five or six years ago with a small herd and has been doing pretty good. Crown's been here in the basin the longest, likely ten years or so, I reckon. Anyway,' turning back to Fagan, he went on, 'that's just about everybody that's anybody in or around the basin.'

Knowing he'd asked all the questions he dared, Fagan brought things to a halt by standing up. Wincing a little, he shook his head.

'I'd say that is enough medicinal liquor for me. My empty stomach is telling me it's been a long time since I had my morning coffee,' then remembering, he frowned. 'And my pony's been standing out there as hungry as I am. Lordy, wouldn't my pa take me down a notch if he knew.'

The blacksmith laughed and, leaving the doctor behind, followed Fagan outside.

'You don't mind, I'll join you for supper. The only place to eat is over at the hotel. Food's usually good and they always put out plenty of it.'

'Sounds like a deal to me. I'll give my horse a bait of oats and a rub down and meet you there.'

★　★　★

As sore and stiff as he was, it only took a few minutes to take care of the dun and after dropping his bedroll in one of the rooms at the hotel, Fagan walked across the lobby and into the restaurant.

Marchal was right, the food was good. Finishing his pan-fried steak, mashed potatoes and fresh green peas, Fagan leaned back in his chair savoring a second cup of coffee.

'You've got yourself a nice, quiet little town here.'

'Yeah. Most times it is a good place to be. Least ways it has been up until recently. But to be honest, not much happens here. It's a small town and there ain't much in the way of social life. Miss Abigail is about the only single woman outside of Mary Ellen Turnbull and they're both too young for me.'

'Well, that Abigail is certainly a prize. Who's the other one?'

'Mary Ellen? She's the daughter of old man Silas Turnbull. Nice enough but, well, guess being raised on a cattle ranch by a pa who thinks she's a he and treats her like a boy, you can't expect her not to turn out a tad strong minded. Now Miss Abigail, she's a regular lady. Got some highfaluting ideas, she has, but for all of that, she's special.'

'Yeah, and according to your Mister Peeters, you're not the only one who thinks that way.'

Marchal laughed. 'Every man within fifty miles of Short Creek's been in love with Miss Abigail at one time or another. Least ways since she grew out of pigtails. That tenderfoot, though. He's taken it on hisself to cut everyone else out. Well, she's too fine a lady for any of the local men folk anyhow.'

'For such a small town, Short Creek has some excitement to it,' Fagan laughed, motioning to the waitress for more coffee. 'On one hand there's the easterner and Miss Abigail and then the possibility of cattle being rustled. How certain do you think Mister Peeters claim on the store owner's daughter really is?'

'I reckon he'll come out ahead. Old man Duniway was one of the first to open up for business here and I wasn't far behind. In all that time I've gotten to know our Miss Abigail. Now, mind you, I ain't talking any against her, but, well, I figured a long time ago that she'd take her first chance to get outa town.' Studying the coffee in his cup, the blacksmith shook his head. 'There never was a day she was gonna take up with some cowhand and raise his kids out on a hard scrabble bit of range. She's had her sights on a big city life since the first time she heard stories from the drummers coming to her pa's store. I do hope she won't be disappointed.'

'What about the rustling? Are the ranches really missing a lot of stock?'

Marchal frowned into his empty dinner plate. 'Well, nobody knows for sure. You gotta understand. You take a big spread like Crown, they don't really know how many head they got. Except at roundup time, and then its only a guess of what they figure should be out there. For some time now there's been talk about cattle going missing. Nobody's been able to prove anything, but . . . well, not too long back old Silas out at the Box M started talking about how he's been missing some stock, too. Can't really tell how many, though.

There's some mighty rugged country back there, up against the badlands and until all the stock is choused out, ain't no way of telling how many critters there are.'

'Yeah, I've seen country like that down south,' Fagan nodded.

'The Box M's got good water and rough as that back country is, there's good graze.'

'So Crown thinks its missing stock and the Box M might be. Who's doing the taking?'

'Nobody knows and everybody's been pretty careful not to point the finger at anyone local. Nope, I'd say it could as easily be a gang of rustlers hiding back in the badlands. But nobody knows for certain.'

'And there's no head count until the next roundup,' Fagan mused. 'That means a lot of last season's yearlings could've been run down to the railhead and nobody'd miss them until they make a gather.'

'Yep, and the trails south are wide

open year round, and so is the trail up through the pass. It'd be rougher, but it's still possible, I guess. It'd be hard to move a herd across Crown land down to the railhead without being seen. Ah, well, it could be anyone or it could be all worry over nothing. It might be that there ain't been any young stuff taken from their mothers.'

'But nobody believes that, do they,' Fagan mused.

'Naw, everyone's waiting. The late spring roundup of yearlings is about to happen out at Crown and Nixon is saying he'll know when they get a tally what's happening.'

'What about the young greenhorn who worked me over, isn't he the head honcho?'

'Winston Peeters?' Marchal chuckled. 'Not likely. He came out here about a year ago. It took two wagons to haul all his boxes and suitcases from the station down at Golden up to the main house. Nobody saw too much of him for a while then one day he came riding in, all tall and proud on the back of a big black horse, all prancing and jigging. Rode up the street and turned around and came back. Stepped out of his saddle, a Mex saddle with a high-backed cantle and all covered with silver doodads, and went into the saloon. Took a look around, sniffed and went back out. Didn't say a word, nose kinda stuck up in the air like he was smelling something rotten. Then he went into the store and that was it. He met Miss Abigail and you saw a changed man. She can do that to a man, I reckon.'

The two men smiled, thinking about it.

'But,' the smithy went on after a moment, 'for all that, he don't know anything about anything, just spends a lot of time over at the store. Leaves the horse at the ranch and comes in on that small wagon of his, hoping to get Miss Abigail to go for a ride, I figure. She does, sometimes, but not often. Naw, it's that Nixon what runs things. Has for years. A hard man, too. Built like a water tank, big and square. Probably weighs 250 pounds and I'd say there's little fat on his frame. And tough. Has to be to run the crew he's got. More tough men. There's even a few what wears their belt guns tied down and loose. Not your usual cowhands, although most of the crew are just that.'

'Sounds like a mean bunch to be stealing beef from.'

'Yeah, and that's why some fingers always seems to get pointed in that direction. Just about as natural, there's some folks think it might be someone over at the Box M. But, hells bells, if people'd think about it they'd know old Silas has got no call to steal another man's cattle. The Box M's the perfect place. Good graze, year-round water and that mix of longhorn and shorthorn he's been building on, there's no reason for him to be taking Crown cattle.'

5

Still sore and stiff from the beating he'd taken, Fagan got a good eight hours of sleep that night, sinking deep in a down-filled mattress. After a breakfast of fried ham, hash browns and eggs cooked the way he liked them, he walked down to check on his horse.

'Hey, there. Wait up a minute,' the old man running the place called out as the cowboy ambled through the wide-open doors. 'Heard tell you was smart-talking Miss Duniway. Don't know if'n I want the business of men what'd do that.'

Fagan stopped, glancing over to a dark, shadowy tack room. Standing with hands on his hips, he waited until the old timer pulled himself out of a rickety looking rocking chair and strode over to stand looking up at the taller man.

The serious look in the stable-hand's eyes stopped Fagan from laughing. Standing a thin whisker over five feet, the sun-reddened face was staring up at the cowboy. It was clear; the old man was mad clear through. This was a serious matter.

Taking his time, Fagan looked the old man up one side and down the other before, pursing his lips, he nodded.

'Yep, I reckon I'd feel the same way if what you heard was true. Fact is who ever told that tall tale is likely to have to answer for it. Since I've been in your fair community I've been called a liar, been beaten up and now learn I'm disrespectful of the most beautiful woman I've ever seen.' Easing his Colt a little in its holster, Fagan let his deep frown grow. 'Now if you'll just point out the jasper that's telling tall tales about something he don't know anything about, I'll have a word with him.'

The wrinkled sunburned face paled a little and the old man stepped back a step or two. 'Wal, now, there ain't no cause for that.'

'Yes, I'd say there was. If someone is spreading tales about me, I'd say that was cause for me to be interested, wouldn't you say?'

'It's just something someone hinted at — '

Fagan didn't let him finish. 'Nope. There were only three people in that store at the time, the young lady, the Easterner and myself. Nobody else would know what was said. So why don't you tell me who is spreading rumors about me.'

'Look, mister, if you say you didn't mistreat Miss Duniway, then you didn't. Forget I said anything.'

Fagan didn't look away, staring the old man in the eye for a long moment.

'I'll say this. You tell whoever's talking out of their hat to stop and I'll let it ride. But if anyone, any single person says one more thing about what didn't happen, if anyone so much as looks cross-eyed at me, then I'll be back. That's when you'll tell me whose putting black on my name and I'll correct the situation.' Once again he lifted his Colt and let it drop back into the leather.

'Now, I'm going to let my horse out into your back corral and I don't want to hear another word from you, understand?'

'Yes, sir. I do hear what you're saying,' the old timer whimpered, backing up before hurrying back into the dusty tack room.

Back on the hotel porch, Fagan took a chair and leaning it against the wall, settled in, not feeling much pride in the tongue lashing he'd given the old man.

★ ★ ★

Maybe, he thought after a while, another day or two would ease the stiffness in his body and he'd ride on about his business. That would give him time to figure out how he was going to get a handle on things. Anyway, doing any riding with his ribs taped up wouldn't be comfortable. Plus if there was talk floating around, another day or two wouldn't hurt. Rumors of someone bad-mouthing a fine woman could spread far and wide and it'd be a good thing to not look like he was running from it.

★ ★ ★

The next morning, after another big breakfast, Fagan still hadn't come up with a plan, so he thought of the old rule, 'when in doubt do nothing' and found a chair on the hotel porch. Sitting with his feet up on the porch railing, he watched the town come alive. Relaxing, he rolled a smoke and scraping a match against the sole of one boot, lit it. For the first time since suffering the beating he felt pretty good and thought he'd probably live to fight another day.

Earlier, while shaving, he'd pulled the tape off the cut over his eyebrow, pulling hair with it, and saw the wound was healing. A small cut, it likely wouldn't even leave a scar. Funny, he thought, thinking back to the remains of the shirt he'd been wearing when being worked over by the tenderfoot, how much blood would flow out of such a little cut. That shirt had gone into the trash and before leaving town he'd have to go replace it. Thinking about going into the store and seeing Miss Duniway brought a smile to his thin lips.

Late in the morning, as he was making up his mind about going in for a cup of coffee, he spotted a bunch of riders coming across the bridge over the river. While the town had been named for the creek that came out of the badlands over to the west, it sat right at where that shallow flow of water met up with the Blue River.

Fagan figured the riders coming across the wide timber bridge from the east to be Crown men. They were all mounted on fine riding stock, every horse in the bunch was big with thick ropy muscle fluid under healthy looking, smooth hide.

In a group the men tied to the hitching rail in front of the hotel and come up on the porch. Fagan nodded when the leader, a big barrel of a man, stepped up, and without giving any sign he'd seen the seated cowboy, pushed through the doors. The next man, Fagan noticed, glared at him as he strode past. The third man, a youngster to look at him, was pulling his riding gloves off but halted when he saw Fagan.

'Well, so this is the big man?' the young man sneered, his upper lip lifted in a look filled with scorn. 'Elias Fagan. The story around the bunkhouse was that you're in town. Don't remember me, do ya.' It was a statement, not a question.

Fagan sat back and slowly looked the man over. This, he saw, was one of the men Marchal described as not being a cowhand. A pair of Colts, their pearl handles splayed out in tied-down holsters, hung heavily from narrow hips. A fancy dresser, the young man's shirt was shiny black silk fastened with slick white buttons. A soft gray Stetson hung down his back on a braided black thong.

Shaking his head, Fagan smiled as his eyes traveled from boots to thick black hair needing a haircut.

'Nope,' he said after a moment. 'Don't see any reason I should, either.'

The gunslinger's eyes hardened at the words, spoken in a soft drawl. Slouching, he let his hands rest on the butts of his two pistols.

Snarling through thin lips, the youngster tried to make his tone threatening. Fagan had to work not to laugh. 'I wasn't riding with Black Jack Ketchum the day you shot him down. If'n I had been there the outcome might have been different. He was a pard of mine. I'm Little Bill Raidler,' he said proudly.

'Don't think I ever heard of you, boy,'

Fagan drawled out his words, emphasizing the last word.

Raidler's body tensed as his fingers began to curl around the gun butts. Before he could speak, Fagan went on with a question.

'You saying you rode with Ketchum and his gang?'

The gun hand glared and then let his body relax. 'Now that wouldn't be smart, would it? Admitting to having been part of a known outlaw bunch? I'm just saying, you might have gotten lucky that day in Jackson County. Woulda been different had I been there.'

Nodding, Fagan slowly unwound from the chair and standing tall looked down into the washed-out blue eyes of the shorter man, forcing him to take a step back. Fagan quickly stepped forward and flicking the thong off the hammer of his own Colt, smiled.

'Are you looking toward a long life or do you want to see just how different things really are?'

Raidler quickly stepped aside, holding up both hands. 'Are you crazy,' he asked in a shrill voice.

'Nope. Just wanted to see how unruffled you really are.' Fagan slumped back against the porch railing. 'So you didn't ride with the Hole-In-The-Wall gang. What're you doing here? Ah, foolish question, it's obvious. You've taken a riding job at Crown. Must be quite a comedown for you, going from being an almost famous gunny to take your place as just another cowherder.'

'I'm not a hired hand,' Raidler snarled having got back his bravado. 'I get paid mighty good for my guns and don't you worry, I'm worth every penny of it.' Turning, he pushed through the batwing doors, disappearing into the saloon.

Fagan chuckled and hooking a toe, pulled his chair back into place. Someday, he knew he'd tease the wrong man and have to back up his words. But today wasn't the day and certainly not with that tinhorn.

Relaxed again, he studied the busy street. Getting closer to noon, the number of mounted riders and wagons had grown. Many of the wagons carried families, with women and men calling and waving to each other. Thinking about it, he suddenly realized that it was Saturday. That would mean many of the families living in the outlying areas were coming in to do their weekly shopping and socializing. Another good reason to sit and watch the town unfold.

Slowly, as the morning sun made its way high in the pale blue sky, the main street of the town filled with horses and wagons. Fagan sat and watched as one ranch wagon pulled up in front of the general store and two men climbed down. There was something about the way the youngest of the pair moved that caught his eye. The older man said something before, with a little wave of a hand, he turned to walk across the street, obviously heading for the saloon.

It was when the other pushed into the store that he realized it was a woman, not a young man. Frowning in thought, he tried to recall what the blacksmith had told him. It came to him and the frown eased into a faint smile. That, he said to himself, would be the Turnbulls from the Box M.

Without giving Fagan a glance, the man stomped up the steps and went into the saloon. Dropping his feet to the porch, the cowboy rose again from the chair and, settling his hat, nodded. Maybe it was time for a drink before he went for coffee.

★ ★ ★

It wasn't as quiet as he expected when he stepped through the half-doors and let them swing behind him.

'So, tell us, old man,' a loud voice called from down toward the back of the room, 'hear you been complaining about losing some of your fancy beeves. Now we all know there's only your little piddling outfit and Crown that's shipping beef anyway regular. So that makes it look like you're blaming your losses on Crown. That don't set well with some of us.'

The Box M owner stood facing the back mirrors, studiously ignoring the taunts coming from the group of men at the other end of the bar.

'Naw,' another, louder voice cut in, 'it ain't right to be putting that name on him. Not less'n ya give him a chance to tell how it really is.' Fagan saw it was the hand that had given him a hard look that was talking. 'Go ahead, Turnbull. What'd ya have to say? Spit it out. You saying someone from Crown is rustling your stock?'

Turnbull didn't take his eyes off the dirt-streaked mirror and was taking a sip of his whiskey when Fagan stepped up to stand next to him.

'Mind if I join you?'

The cattleman put his glass down and glanced sideways.

'Who are you?'

'Name's Fagan, Elias Fagan. I rode into town a couple days ago.'

'Ah, yeah, I heard something about you. Well, thanks just the same, but I don't need anyone to fight my battles. Those troublemakers will get tired of trying to bait me in a bit.'

'Hey, Turnbull,' someone called from down the bar. 'Hired yourself a big gun, have ya?' Fagan glanced down and saw it was the thin, fancy gun, Raidler, making the noise. Smiling, he motioned to the bartender.

'How about a glass of your coldest beer, partner.'

'I don't want no trouble in here, stranger.' Otto said, not moving.

Fagan nodded and stepped away from the bar.

'All right,' he said loud enough for his voice to carry across the room. 'If that's the way it's to be, let's start this dance. You,' he pointed, 'the young gunslinger there. Yeah, you with those fancy pistols wrapped around your belly, I'm talking to you. Outside on the porch I made you back water. Either show us how fast you really are or shut up. And to be fair, I'm telling you now, you just aren't fast enough. Now,' he went on, dropping his voice so only the bartender could hear but not taking his eyes off Raidler, 'by the time this is settled, there had better be a glass of beer sitting on the bar right next to Mr Turnbull.' Speaking up again, he called out, 'Well, what's it gonna be, tinhorn?'

The big man who had to be the foreman, Nixon, was sitting with a couple other men at one of the tables and had been taking it all in. Coming slowly to his feet he raised both hands and stepped in front of Raidler and faced Fagan.

'Better be playing it easy, mister,' the big man's voice was harsh and filled with authority. He was, Fagan thought, used to men cringing when he spoke.

'Oh, I doubt the two-gun terror is as bad or as fast as he thinks he is.'

Nixon frowned and took a step toward Fagan. 'I wasn't thinking of just

Raidler. Now you'll notice I'm not packing iron. Was you to shuck those Colts, I'd be showing you how a real man settles things.'

Fagan laughed loudly. 'Why would I want to do that? Brawling in a saloon isn't my style. Nope, I guess not. But if you come on too strong, with your loud brag, someone will most certainly get hurt.'

For a long moment the two men stared at each other. No one in the room moved while they waited. Then, sounding as if it came from the bottom of an empty rain barrel, the big ranch foreman laughed.

'Yeah, and it ain't my style to buck a stranger wearing a heavy six-gun. But anyway, there ain't no call for you to get involved. The boys was just funning Turnbull. That's no reason for anyone getting hurt. Go ahead and enjoy your beer and we'll forget the whole thing. What d'ya say?'

Fagan stood for a long minute, his gun hand resting on his gun butt.

Finally nodding, he turned his back to the group and reached for the beer.

'Now that sounds almost friendly,' he called over his shoulder. 'But not too smart. Man might get hurt some, coming between and betwixt like that.'

Picking up his beer glass with his left hand he turned back to look into the mirror.

★　★　★

'You took quite a chance there,' Turnbull said, keeping his voice low. 'Word is that that skinny one is real fast. And Nixon has killed more than one man with those fists of his.'

'I don't doubt it, he's big enough and I figure mean enough. As for the gun slick, well, he may be fast but all he knows about me is that I took on a couple of his partners a while back. He doesn't know if I did it from the front or back. Anyway, we can now do as the big man says, enjoy our drinks in peace and quiet.'

'Fagan,' Turnbull said after a moment. 'I once knew a fella named Fagan. That'd be a number of years ago, back down in the Texas border country before I came up here. He had a spread and I bought a small bunch of longhorns from him. As I recall his name was Fagan. Ranch had a Mex name, I can't remember what it was. You be any relation to him?'

'Well, that sounds like Pa. The home place is the Cibolo Creek Ranch. Are you still running longhorns?' he asked, changing the subject.

'Nope, I brought in a few Durham bulls from Chicago. They cross-breed pretty good and produce a heavier animal.'

'That's what Pa did. The longhorn is a tough beast but tends to put on weight slow. That's one good thing coming from England, their shorthorn breed of cattle.'

Turnbull chuckled. 'I heard you had a little run-in with our local piece of royalty. From what I heard, you came in second best in that match-up.'

Fagan shook his head. 'I guess you could say that. I know I'm still bandaged from belly button to armpit. Most of the stiffness is gone but there're still some colorful bruises, I expect.' Wanting to talk about something else, he put on his serious face. 'The blacksmith and I got to talking and he doesn't think much of the story that you're rustling Crown beef. Why is it that Crown's men are talking it up?'

'Don't know. Just feeling their oats, I reckon. Boy, if I'd known there'd someday be trouble, I might have looked elsewhere when I went looking for land. Just getting to be too darn much trouble.'

'I hear you haven't been here as long as Crown.'

'No, they was here when I rode in but that piece above the creek and beyond the river had been a little spread that went broke. I think the fella before me tried to get bigger than he should have and couldn't make it. My getting away from longhorns is what's going to make the Box M successful. I got good land with plenty of year-round water, good graze and protected some from any harsh winter storms. There's somewhat short of sixty-five thousand acres but that's enough if I can produce quality beef. That's all a man could ask for, I reckon.'

Motioning to Otto for another drink, the old rancher looked Fagan over. 'What brought you to Short Creek, anyway?'

Fagan shook his head slowly. 'Your having a growing herd that seems to be shrinking in numbers. That isn't exactly what Marshall Goodall down in Golden told me but close.'

For a moment Turnbull just stared up at the cowboy. Keeping his voice low, he frowned. 'What do you know about the marshal?'

'Well, I was just riding through Golden when I had a little talk with him. I delivered a herd up to Abilene for Pa and just kept riding. I've been doing that since I left the home ranch a few years ago. Went out to see what California was all about, worked for a while up in Wyoming, even rode shotgun for Wells Fargo once or twice. I guess I'm looking for something. Don't know what it is exactly, though.'

'And?'

'And I stopped in to see Goodall. He knew I'd worn a badge up in Wyoming and when I mentioned my plan to ride on north, he asked me to stop here in Short Creek and look around. Seems he'd been questioning a small jag of cattle that'd been herded to the loading pens. Mostly beef carrying the Crown brand, he said, but with a few Box M markings. The buyer had a bill of sale that appeared all right and proper so the marshal couldn't say much but he didn't think it was on the up and up. From what he told me, you'd sent him a telegram asking for help.'

The ranch owner nodded. 'Yeah, I did, but nothing came of it.'

'Well, he's having some problems

down in that end of the country and can't get away. He sort of asked me to stop by and see what the trouble was. See if I could give you some help.'

'Well, that does sound like music to my ears,' Turnbull muttered. 'It really started a few months ago when my foreman, Caldwell, became convinced we were losing cattle. Short Creek isn't big enough to have its own law so I wired the marshal.'

Neither man said anything for a brief time, both looking for answers in the bottom of their drinks.

Glancing sideways at Fagan, Turnbull spoke first. 'You say that Crown gunny knows about you? Where from?'

'Ah, it was while I was deputy sheriffing up in Wyoming. I had a run-in with a few of his friends one afternoon. They were part of the Hole-In-The-Wall gang. Came into town and hit the bank. When they came out we were ready. Young Raidler claimed a couple of them were his friends but when I offered to let him get revenge he backed down. Of course, we were standing belly to belly at the time.'

'That close both of you'd get shot.'

Fagan chuckled. 'I didn't think he'd stand for it, and he didn't.'

Turnbull went back to staring into the back mirror giving Fagan an opportunity to look the man over.

'You wouldn't be open to hiring another hand, now would you?' he asked after a while.

'I dunno,' Turnbull answered. 'What do you have in mind?'

'Well, if I'm going to be looking around, it probably wouldn't do to have everyone know what I was doing. Coming up, someone took a shot at me,' he stopped when the older man shot a questioning look at him. 'Naw, whoever it was just wasn't up to the job. I don't have any reason to think anyone up here knows about me, other than that I'm drifting through. So if I hired on, it'd give me a reason to do whatever I need to do.'

The rancher leaned on his elbows

and thought about it for a moment. 'That makes a lot of sense. And yes, I could use a good man. I lost my foreman recently. Karl Caldwell just up and took off one day. He and a couple of the hands had come into town one Saturday afternoon. The hands came back late that night but Caldwell didn't. I think Nixon got to him, but can't prove it. Anyway, I've got six hands but none of them wants the job. I could use the help; at least until the spring roundup is done. Hell, with the spring roundup coming, I could use another half-dozen men.'

Glancing sideways, he studied Fagan's face. 'Got to tell you, though, both taking on that job and looking into any rustling, well, it could be dangerous. There's been too much talk about night riders. Nobody seems to know anything for sure, but . . . well. I figure all the talk that's been going around will come home to roost and that's when Nixon will come calling. He'll have to have someone to lay the blame on or his

New York owners will be asking questions. Looks like I'm the only one available. I reckon that's what his men were doing just now; starting to make everyone think the Box M is doing the rustling.'

'You think Nixon is behind it?'

'I don't know. But I do know nobody from the Box M is stealing cattle and who does that leave? There are a few small ranches and farms trying to make a go of it down south a bit, trying to prove up on some of that open range. It's unlikely any of them are involved. It could be someone from outside I suppose. That's hard to believe, though. There hasn't been too many new faces riding into town this past winter. They'd surely be noticed. Except for you, that is. I reckon that's the same thinking Nixon's doing.'

The ranch owner shook his head, studying the bottom of his glass. 'All I know is what everybody knows, there's word that a lot of Crown beef have been missing. I know nobody from the

Box M has anything to do with it. But there it is.'

'Well, it's clear someone is moving beef they don't own. That's what Marshal Goodall asked me to look into, to ride up here to Short Creek and see what I could find out.'

Fagan finished his beer and thought about the offer. 'So, I'll tell you what,' he said finally, 'I'll take the job for a few months. At least until the tally is completed. But I have to warn you, most of my work will be finding out about the rustling.'

'I'd appreciate it. Thank you. I only hope it doesn't end up with you getting hurt.'

'Sure fire, from the welcome I got since I rode in, things can only get better.'

6

Getting his gear from the hotel room, Fagan saddled his horse and rode over to meet his new boss at the general store. He smiled at the thought of seeing the beautiful storekeeper once more. He had been staying away from the store, thinking he'd better not run into the fellow from back east again, at least not until his ribs healed. But it wasn't to be. As he walked his horse toward the ranch wagon, he saw Turnbull finishing the job of tying down the boxes of supplies. The other person, Mary Ellen he figured, was already sitting on the wagon's bench seat.

'Ah, Fagan. You're just in time,' the rancher smiled as he gathered the reins and settled on to the seat. 'Here, let me introduce you to my daughter. Mary Ellen, this here's Elias Fagan. I've hired him to ramrod the place, leastwise until after the roundup.'

'What? Father, you can't be serious,' Fagan liked the sound of her angry voice. Without glancing his way, she went on scolding her father. 'He's the one Mister Peeters had a run-in with. He's nothing but a drifter. You don't know anything about him.' Turning finally to face Fagan, she shook her head.

Fagan let a thin smile lift his lips. Mary Ellen's tanned brown face held a dark look as she glared fiercely at him, her black eyes flashing with anger. 'You are not welcome at the Box M. Whatever my father told you, you can forget. Just keep riding. Nobody in the basin wants you here.'

Chuckling softly, the mounted cowboy kept his voice soft. 'Why, ma'am, that's the friendliest thing I've heard since riding into town. I sure do thank you. Now, if your father wants to fire me, then he can and I'll go about my business. But he's the only one that I'll listen to on the matter.'

Silas Turnbull's laugh only made his daughter's anger grow.

'Nicely said, young man, nicely said. Now, Mary Ellen, the day hasn't come that you're running the Box M, not yet at least. We need a good strong man on the place for the next month or two and I think this is the one. Least ways, far as I can see, he's the only one. You just sit back now, and let's get this show on the road.' Looking over at Fagan he nodded. 'Let's ride.'

* * *

After crossing the bridge over the river, Fagan rode along behind as the wagon turned away and bumped along the ranch road toward the bluffs. Fagan let the wagon get ahead of him and even then stayed out of the billowing dust by riding off to one side.

Tall skinny cottonwoods, willows and brush lined both banks of the meandering creek, giving way to tall grasses a short distance from the waterway. Looking over the land as the little party followed the twin ruts of the track, Fagan was paying close attention to the condition of the graze and closer attention to the few head of cattle that was feeding in the lush grasses. For the most part, the cattle were fatter than the average longhorn. Mostly deep reddish brown in color and heavier, especially in the shoulders, the English shorthorn breed was clearly evident.

For most of the afternoon they followed along the creek bottom until, angling away, they started the long, slow climb toward the towering bluffs that filled the western sky. Where the wagon road had been mostly across flat land, it now started to make a series of switchbacks as it first dropped down into a wide ravine only to climb another series up the other side. Looking up toward the sheer face of the bluffs, Fagan noted how the ravine narrowed and became choked with mesquite brush. Shaking cattle out of there would be hard, dirty and often dangerous work.

After crossing three or four such gullies, each really a minor canyon, the road turned up and became steeper. The ranch buildings came into view just as the sun was nearing the top of the western bluffs. Set high on the side of the ravine, the big log ranch house faced east, providing a view over the flats and beyond that Fagan thought would be spectacular.

Out of sight until climbing the last few hundred feet was a series of barns and stock pens. A smoke house and other out-buildings angled off to one side. A covered dogtrot connected the end of the main house to a long, low, shake-roofed building in the other direction. This, Fagan figured, would be the bunkhouse.

Two men, both bandy-legged cowboys, ambled from the bunk house when Silas Turnbull pulled to a stop near the back door of the main house. Neither man hid their surprise when

Fagan swung down.

'Moses, Cletus, I want you to meet Elias Fagan,' Turnbull said. 'I've hired him to fill in Karl's place, at least through the roundup.'

The men just nodded their greetings. Fagan noticed that Mary Ellen had climbed down unaided and without a word strode into the house.

After lending a hand carrying the supplies into the house and leaving everything on counters and the long table in the kitchen for the cook to put away, the men walked the animals over toward the barn. Slowly, as they unhitched the team and Fagan unsaddled his dun horse, the men started talking, being careful not to ask any pointed questions but trying to learn what they could about the stranger.

★　★　★

Over the next week or so Fagan got to know the men and the layout of the ranch. Only once or twice did he talk with Silas Turnbull, but not once did he see any sign of the old man's daughter, Mary Ellen.

The hands were at first very cautious, until one of them, an older man named Henshaw, remembered something about the Cibolo Creek Ranch.

'Now that name sounds familiar,' Henshaw said, slapping down his cards one night after supper when he, Moses, Fagan and a young man called Lefty were playing poker. Using match sticks for counters, the four had been playing draw poker and discussing this, that and the other thing, as men would. Lefty, it was explained, was called that, but not because he was left-handed. No, the name was given to him because of his clumsy ways, acting like he had two left feet.

'I heard you say you been out to California,' Lefty said at one point, throwing in his cards. 'I hope you had better luck in the gold fields than I'm having with these cards.'

Lefty was probably closer to his age,

Fagan thought, but somehow seemed to be a lot younger. Moses, on the other hand, was almost as old as Turnbull, least ways he looked like he was.

Everybody laughed and the game continued. 'Nope,' Fagan said after the cards had been dealt. 'Working in some creek filled with ice cold water hoping to pick out enough gold to make it worth while didn't look like fun to me. I didn't stay long before going on down to the Cuidad de Los Angeles. Pa had some friends down there I wanted to meet up with.'

Moses dealt the next hand and as the betting started, commented on his visit to California. 'Yeah, I been there. Right after things started settling down up in the gold country. Most of those fellas what found their fortunes had cleaned up and there wasn't much left for us late-comers. You was down south? Reckon you saw some of those big Mexican rancheros, then.'

Fagan discarded two cards, peeked at the replacements and smiled. 'Uh huh.

Pa's friend, Don Diego Rodriguiz de Gomez has a rancho down near the border. You know much about Mexican *caballeros?*'

'Some of the best men with a lariat I ever did see. Yeah, I'll take three cards.'

'Good horsemen, too,' Henshaw offered, cussing under his breath as he threw in his hand.

The betting went around with Lefty laying down two pair, taking the pot. Pulling the small stack of matches his way, he looked up at Fagan.

'Your pa have a ranch down there?'

'No. His place is over in west Texas.'

'What's it like?'

'The Cibolo Creek Ranch? A lot like what Turnbull's doing here, a mix of longhorn and English shorthorn. Pa was there right after the war with Mexico and staked out enough land to make it work. He runs mostly cattle with a few horses.'

'Cibolo Creek Ranch, now that sounds like something I heard before,' Henshaw murmured, pushing his small pile of matches in to the center of the table. 'I'll bet, let's see,' counting, 'twenty-three matches.'

'I'll call,' Fagan counted out his bet, 'and raise you ten more.'

'I'm light,' Henshaw said, 'anyone loan me a few? I've got a winning hand here.'

Moses nodded and pushed a handful his way.

'What did happen to your last foreman,' Fagan asked, showing he had three queens and taking the pot.

'Dunno,' Moses said. 'Last anyone saw of him was in town, at the saloon. Nobody was paying much attention, I guess. When me'n Lefty had our fill, we looked around but didn't see him anywheres. Figured he'd gone without us. That was his way. Always the boss, ya know. Never overly friendly.'

Fagan nodded. He'd known crew bosses and foremen like that, men who thought they could get more out of their men if they didn't get too friendly with them.

'Mister Turnbull says he never

showed up at the ranch again. Didn't he pack his war bag?'

'Nope, didn't ever see him again. After a few days someone crammed his belongings into a sack and tossed it on to that bunk back of the room. If'n he comes back, it's all there. The boss said he'd been paid, we all had, it being end of the month. Mister Turnbull said he figured ol' Caldwell just decided to ride on. Seems funny, but he was a standoffish sorta fella.' he stopped and looking around at the other players. 'I'm calling it quits for the night. Got a lot of riding to do tomorrow.'

★ ★ ★

The Box M range covered a lot of ground and a couple days later Fagan took the opportunity to look over that section that bordered the Blue River. It was while riding with Henshaw to drop supplies at the closest line shack to what was called the Big Flats that they found Caldwell's body.

7

The Big Flats, Henshaw told Fagan, was Box M's usual holding ground during a roundup.

'Old Turnbull's a pretty smart fella. After buying out the last man what tried, even while he was having the old owner's house and the other buildings worked on, he had men out damming up springs and cleaning out seeps, making ponds for his stock. The one out on that stretch of ground we call Big Flats is more like a small lake. The flat land around it is near perfect for holding a bunch of cattle while the branding is going on. Once a herd is made up, we drive it south to the river. There's a shallow ford that we use. The Box M herd is combined with that of Crown's and the drive is made south to the rail yards in Golden. It's something the old man got Nixon to agree to early on. Up to now, it's worked pretty slick, the two ranches working together on the drive south to the railhead at Golden.'

The two riders had pulled up on a low ridge to give the heavily loaded pack horse a breather and after passing a tobacco sack back and forth, sat enjoying the morning sunshine and their smoke.

'See off there?' Henshaw was pointing at what looked like a broad strip of dark silver in the distance. 'That's the Blue River. It's pretty wide and shallow along there. About the last place ya can push a herd over before getting on the trail through the pass. River gets pretty fast and furious from then on up on to the bench. Can't see it, but on that way,' he gestured with a thumb the other direction, 'it curves around a bit and where the creek meets up with it, is town.'

Fagan sat silently smoking and looking around, trying to get an idea of where things were.

In the far distance he could see the blue haze of a low mountain range.

'That the Mogul Mountains?' he asked nodding in that direction.

'Sure is. The Blue River gets its start up there. Where it flows through there's a sorta low pass. It's a steep ride and not much on the other side, just high desert country. About twenty miles of it to get to any country worth while.'

Fagan slouched back in the saddle and tried to picture in his mind the map he'd seen of this part of the country. That map, hanging on the wall in Marshal Goodall's office, had been produced by the Denver and Union Pacific Railroad. At the time he hadn't paid much attention but he'd noticed a narrow-gauge rail line coming down from the mining country up north in Montana but as he recalled that would be farther west. Somewhere on the other side of the lava badlands, he figured. Thinking about that, he wondered if that line was being used by the rustlers.

According to Henshaw, that wasn't likely.

'Naw. That's just a little feeder line from farther up north, hooking up with the Denver and Union Pacific line on down at Golden. Turnbull and me rode back up behind the main house into the badlands once, looking if there was a trail through there. We couldn't find anything that looked likely. Might be farther down south, but up in this end it's all rough and filled with a series of deep, jagged gullies and canyons.'

'Now, that big flat piece of ground down there,' again Henshaw was pointing this time to a level stretch a mile or so from the river, 'that's the Big Flats.'

'Has there ever been any trouble between the ranches once the herds are combined?'

'Naw. Ever since we've been doing it that way, everybody's right neighborly. Nixon keeps a tight rein on his men. Usually he's got twenty or more men working their roundup. We simply swim

100

our market stock across the river and they get mixed into the Crown stock. It all comes out when the herd is tallied by the buyer down at the loading pens.' Chuckling to himself, he went on. 'And once we get shet of the herd at the loading pens, there's a night of howling at one of the saloons. That's what all the hands look forward to. The ride back can be something but I don't ever remember any fights or anything.'

The two men sat, warmed by the sun and lost in their own thoughts for a time, then being careful to pinch the fire from their quirlys, gigged their horses down off the ridge.

Sitting the saddle on the ranch horse, a big high-stepping sorrel, Fagan was busy scanning the range they were riding through, marking in his mind various landmarks. This habit was typical of men used to riding far distances and done unconsciously. The landscape was rolling grassland, covered in thick spring bunchgrass and any rider that didn't pay attention stood the chance of getting lost in the sameness of it all. It was the sight of a flock of crows fighting in the distance that Fagan questioned next.

'Hey, Henshaw, is that a waterhole those birds are squabbling about?'

Standing as tall as he could in his stirrups, the older cowboy shook his head. 'Nope. No waterhole I know of over that way. Crows, I reckon. Seems funny, though. If'n its water they was after, there's the whole darn river back there. It ain't much outa our way, let's go take a look. Damn birds're scavengers and it could be a calf in trouble.'

★ ★ ★

The birds had been at work for some time, Fagan figured looking down at the remains of what had been a man. Likely coyotes and other varmints, too, he thought. All that was left was bones and most of them had been scattered. Rocks that had been piled over the body had been pushed aside and now did no more than hold down bits and pieces of ripped clothing. Whoever he'd been, his makeshift grave hadn't lasted long.

The crows had flown when the men and their horses rode up, loudly protesting the interruption. For a time the two men sat their saddles, looking at their find. Finally, sighing, Henshaw climbed wearily out of the saddle.

Nudging aside a couple of the larger rocks that had covered the dead man's arm, he cussed. 'Ah, dammit all to hell, that bit of shirt,' Henshaw murmured, not taking his eyes off the arm, 'looks like what Caldwell was wearing into town.'

Fagan stepped down and helped the cowboy move the remaining rocks. Picking up a large piece of the blue cotton material that had been held down by the rocks, he poked a finger through a small hole.

'About the size of a bullet, wouldn't you say?'

Henshaw's answer was more cuss words.

'Now, who in hell would do that?' he asked after a bit. 'Looks like it's in the back, too.'

'Wonder why he was out here,' Fagan mused, looking around. 'This is a long way from the road to the ranch.'

'Yeah, Big Flat and the river are over that way and that's a good ten miles or more from the bunkhouse.'

'Didn't his horse show up?'

'He was riding one of the ranch animals, but there wasn't any empty saddled horse ever found. That's probably why we all thought he'd just ridden out. Personally, I always thought Nixon or one of his gunhands might've had something to do with Caldwell's leaving.' Looking down at what was left of the foreman, he shook his head. 'And just maybe one of them did.'

'Well, I'd suggest that we put the rocks back as best we can. We can send out a wagon when we get back to the house and bring him in. I suppose there's a ranch burying ground?'

'Yeah, up on the hills above the place. Miss Mary Ellen takes good care of it. That's where her ma's buried. We'll have to notify the marshal down in Golden, too. Won't be much he can do, but he ought to be told, I reckon.'

Fagan thought about that for a minute, then without saying anything, nodded.

* * *

Back at the home place a couple days later, Henshaw drew a rough map of where Caldwell's remains could be found. He and Fagan had discussed who would be the best man to send out with a wagon to bring the bones back. Following Henshaw's suggestion, the job had fallen to Moses.

'He was probably the closest to the foreman of any of us. Least ways having to haul back what's left of Caldwell will likely set with him better'n it would with one of the younger hands.'

Silas Turnbull stood silently by as the

two men described what they had found.

'Why would anyone want to shoot Caldwell?' he asked, his words coming low as he looked blindly at the ground. 'Dammit, I never did really believe he'd just up and ride away. But you say the hole in his shirt was in the back? Why? Caldwell had been on the place a long time. He was a good hand and treated the men fairly. Never had any trouble with him, so why would someone want to gun him down? And,' he went on before anyone could interrupt, looking up and speaking stronger, 'why was he clear out by the Big Flat? That's a good ten miles or more from the road to town. I don't understand it at all.'

No answers to his questions were offered and for long minutes the crew stood around, thinking about the murdered foreman. Finally, slapping his sweat-stained Stetson against a pants leg, Turnbull turned back toward the big house, stopping after a few steps to look back at Fagan.

'Well, we'll bring his body back and put him up on the hill. That's where Mary Ellen's ma is buried, you know,' he said softly. Glancing up at the men, his eyes blinking away any sign of a tear, he nodded. 'It's getting a mite late now, but Fagan, how about you and Henshaw take Mary Ellen into town tomorrow morning early. She's got a list of supplies the cook is wanting and she'll need some help. While you're at it, look around and see if you can hire on six or eight hands. We'll be needing them to start cleaning out the breaks.'

'All right,' said Fagan. 'Should someone send a telegram letting the marshal down in Golden know about Caldwell?'

'Ah, well, I suppose. Won't make any difference but I guess he should be told.'

Warning Moses to take along a shovel and a tarp, Fagan helped him harness up one of the ranch buckboards. The older man had decided to head out, saying something about sleeping out and getting back as soon as he could.

★　★　★

The morning ride into town was uneventful, the two men following behind Mary Ellen Turnbull in a ranch wagon were not bothered by the little bit of dust raised by the single horse. For a while they talked quietly as they rode, with Henshaw describing the layout of the Box M range to the new foreman. Soon, though, that topic had been talked out and the two men rode silently, each in their own thoughts.

'Miss Turnbull,' Henshaw touched the brim of his hat as the young woman pulled up in front of the general store, 'I 'xpect you'll be wanting to have a little chat with Miss Abigail while you gather up your list of things. Me'n Fagan here'll be around looking to see if there's any hands wanting to work. What say we have lunch together over at the hotel in a couple hours?'

Mary Ellen Turnbull let her hard glance center on Fagan. 'Thank you, Henshaw, but I think I'd rather have lunch with Abigail, if you don't mind.'

Scowling her displeasure, she climbed down and, after dropping the reins over a hitch rail, stepped up on to the boardwalk and, without a backward glance, pushed through the door.

Henshaw chuckled. 'Boy, that girl has sure taken a big dislike to you. Wonder what set her off?'

Fagan had to smile. 'I can't figure it out either. Seems to have something to do with her hearing how I'd bad-mouthed her friend, Miss Abigail.'

'Way I heard that, you paid a good price for even talking to her. Yeah, don't look so surprised. Eloy Marchal is by way of being a friend. He told me all about your little tussle with the eastern dude. Well, I reckon that's as good a place as any to start looking for riders. The blacksmith'll know who's in town and who's looking for a few weeks work. We'll try that and then I'll buy you a drink. C'mon.'

Marchal was glad to see Fagan again and, after shaking his head about available men, agreed to taking time off for a drink at the saloon.

'That's the most likely place to find hands, anyhow. Henshaw, I wonder why you didn't start your search there.'

The older cowboy laughed. 'Didn't want the new foreman of the Box M to think that all I wanted was a drink.'

'Ah, so you've move up in the world, have you?' the burly blacksmith said glancing at Fagan over his shoulder as he pushed through the swinging doors of the drinking establishment. 'From one day being a street brawler to soon becoming the new foreman of the second largest ranch in the basin. Now, that's not bad.'

'Who's the new foreman out at the Box M?' a voice called out from down the bar. Four or five men stood in a bunch at the far end. Spread around the long room were others, some sitting around a felt-covered poker table and at a few of the smaller round tables that lined the far wall.

'Ach, so it's news to you, too, Mister Nixon,' Marchal asked. 'I always figured you had your big thick finger on all the news of the area. Let me introduce you to Elias Fagan, boys,' he went on, smiling at the entire room. 'And as such, in his new job, I'm going to let him buy me the first drink of the day.'

Laughing, he dropped a big callous-covered hand heavily on the mahogany bar. 'Otto, my friends here and I will have a glass of your finest whiskey, if you please.'

Fagan smiled as he nodded, spreading a few coins out on the wood. 'I'll stick with a glass of beer,' he said quietly.

'Me'n Mister Fagan already met,' Nixon's voice carried the length of the room, silencing all the other talk. 'Seems maybe Little Billy Raidler was right on the money when he said Turnbull was hiring his own gunmen.'

Fagan shook his head. 'Nope. Just

helping out during the roundup.'

'Well, so what happened to old Caldwell? Old man Turnbull finally get smart and fire him?'

Fagan let his smile fade as he took up his frosty glass with his left hand. After taking a sip of the malty brew, he leaned to look down at the half dozen men standing around the Crown foreman.

'Nope. Someone shot Mister Caldwell, in the back.' Fagan let his words drop into the quiet of the room. Keeping his eyes trained on the small black stones that were Nixon's, he explained in a quiet, serious tone. 'Some backshooter did him in a few weeks ago. We found his body covered with rocks out near Big Flat.'

Nixon's eyes didn't waver.

'So, and I suppose Turnbull is blaming me or one of my men.' Stepping away from the group, the big foreman strode up to stand facing Fagan. 'I been told you carry a badge. Any truth to that?'

Fagan didn't let his eyes waver. 'Once I was a deputy sheriff, but that was up in the Wyoming territory. Right now I'm working for Silas Turnbull and looking for a half-dozen men to hire on for the roundup.'

Nixon had planted his feet and let his hands hang loosely at his side. The expression on his face didn't change as he studied the cowboy. Finally with a little nod, he said his piece.

'Let me tell you how it is, Mister Foreman. Crown and the Box M are making a herd. Your men and mine will be spending the next few weeks chasing the stock out of their winter hideouts. Once that work's done and the branding's been finished we'll be moving both herds south in one drive. Now, me and my men'll run things from there. Crown's got the biggest part of that herd, so all your people have to do is sit back and stay out of our way. Really ain't no call for you all to go along. You understand what I'm saying?'

Fagan, not letting his eyes leave Nixon's face, took another sip of beer and without looking putting his glass back on the bar. Smiling, he slowly shook his head.

'Yep, I understand what you said and that may be the way things were done in the past. But this time we'll be doing our share of the work. I want the cattle buyers in Golden to know these cattle, those wearing both Crown and Box M markings, are being legally sold. Now, do you understand what I'm saying?'

For a long minute the two men, one a little older with specks of gray in his hair and built like a barrel with arms and a chest filling his shirt almost to the tearing point and the other ten years younger, tall and long limbed stared at each other. The silence in the long, dimly lit room was thick enough to cut.

Fagan decided it wouldn't help to get off on the wrong foot, lifted his lips a little in a smile. 'You all have been doing this for a long time and know how best to do it, but I'm not the kind of foreman to sit back and let anyone mistreat my men. That's all.'

Nixon sneered. 'We been working together for a few years and we all know our job. Having two bosses on a drive won't work.'

'Couldn't agree with you more. You ramrod the drive, that's fine with me. I just want everyone to know, the Box M hands will be doing their share of the work. There won't be any sitting back and letting Crown's men take care of things.'

'What're you saying? Spit it out.'

'When it comes to counting cattle and getting them to the buyer, well, we've all heard the rumors about that, haven't we. Every since I rode into town, all I've heard is that both ranches are losing stock, that cattle are being rustled. Seems likely that if anyone is selling cattle on the sly, then there's a buyer or two involved. This way any sale will clearly be on the up and up.'

Nixon's face slowly turned red with

anger. 'Why you . . . are you calling me a rustler?'

'Nope,' Fagan slowly shook his head. 'Once again, nobody's pointing a finger at anyone, so don't go getting up a head of steam unnecessarily. All I'm saying is, I'm taking the Box M money to do a job and that is what I'm going to do. Like it or not, that's the way it will be. And as far as the scum that shot Caldwell goes, no, nobody has yet to point a finger at anyone. Not yet, anyway.'

'You feel pretty safe, don't ya, with that Colt hanging there by your hand. Well, I don't think a real man has to rely on any weapons but those he was born with. I've killed men with my bare fists, men who thought they could tell me, Raleigh Nixon, where to head in. You won't be the first one, I ever catch you without that gun.'

'Oh, well, if that's what it's going to take to get a roundup done, let loose your wolf,' Fagan, using his left hand to unbuckle his gun-belt.

8

'Now wait a cotton picking minute, you two,' Otto ordered, slapping the bar with a bung starter. 'Ain't gonna be no fighting in here. You gonna go at it, take it out in the street where it belongs.'

At that point Marchal stepped in between the two men and held up his hands.

'You two are crazy. You're gonna have to work together whether you like it or not to get the spring roundup going. Crown is big but can't do it all alone, so back off, Nixon. What with all the rumors floating around about someone stealing stock, now ain't the time to go starting trouble.'

'I'll put the boots to anyone calling me a rustler,' the big man snarled.

'Go back to your drinking. Ain't nobody calling anyone anything.'

'I won't be forgetting this, black-smith,' Nixon growled.

The three men stood like that until Fagan, letting his little smile grow, turned back to the bar and picked up his beer glass. As the tension in the room subsided, talk, first quiet but slowly picking up as jokes were shared, was soon back to normal.

Taking their drinks with them, Henshaw, Fagan and the blacksmith moved over to a table against the wall.

'I hear you're looking for men?' one of the men who had been sitting at the poker table stood looking down at Henshaw.

'Rocky, I might have known you'd be around.' Jabbing a thumb in Fagan's direction, he nodded. 'This here's the man to talk to. Fagan's running things out at the ranch now.'

Letting his glance move to Fagan the man made his pitch. 'I'm Cyril Rockfort, Mister Fagan. And I could use a few weeks work. We got the first cutting in and all the new seed planted and there ain't much for us to do for a while.'

'Rocky's got a farm on south of Crauley's B-slash-B. Raises a good crop of winter wheat each spring and usually gets another crop a bit later. Sells it to the ranchers for winter feed. We always get our share. Once he was a top hand, before picking up a shovel and turning farmer,' Henshaw said, teasing the other man.

'Sounds like you've hired on with the roundup before?' said Fagan.

'Yep, helping out at roundup every since I quit cowboying. Since I discovered it was a lot easier to raise a crop than bust my butt in the saddle.'

'We'll be chousing them out of the breaks starting tomorrow morning. Bring your gear and come on out to the ranch.'

Rockfort nodded. 'I'll be there.'

Watching the man walk away smiled and looked arou 'That's one. Think there candidates in here?'

119

'Dunno. There's a couple men sitting back there looking our way. Those at that table there,' he pointed with his chin, 'that's Junior Crauley and a couple B-slash-B hands sitting over there. Probably hiding out from whatever work the old man gave them to do. They won't be looking for work. Anyway, that heavy talk of Nixon's might have scared the others a mite. Let's have another beer and give them a chance to think about it.'

'You two can sit here and do your work,' Marchal said, getting to his feet, 'but I've got a whole lot of horseshoes to shape up. Let me know before you ride out if you need any more men and I'll keep my eyes open.'

★   ★   ★

Fagan and Henshaw had signed on four more men before calling it good and heading over to the hotel for lunch. There was no sign of either Mary Ellen Abigail.

'We get through here,' Henshaw said, not trying to hide his smile, 'and I'll go see how much longer Miss Mary Ellen's going to be.'

'You do that and I'll enjoy the peace and quiet from the hotel porch.'

Setting in one of the rocking chairs, Fagan took the makings from his shirt pocket and slowly rolled a cigarette. Scraping a wooden match along his pants leg to fire it and lighting the twisted end of his quirly, he blew out the flame and flicked the match out into the street.

'Mister Fagan?' a man called from the corner of the porch.

'Yeah?' Fagan looked around to see a middle-aged cowboy standing in the building's shadow. 'What can I do for you?'

'I don't want anyone to see me. Could you step over here?'

Fagan hesitated. As far as he knew Nixon was still in the saloon but it wasn't likely that he would set up an ambush. His way would be to step right in and start slugging it out. 'Yeah,' he finally said, getting up from the chair and walking over to stand looking down at the man.

'My names Sam Collins, Mister Fagan,' he said softly. 'I . . . well, I was one of the men what held you when Mister Peeters beat on you.' Quickly his words came tumbling out. 'He said you'd talked bad to Miss Abigail and had to be taught a lesson. Honest, Mister Fagan, we thought we were doing right. Least I did. The other fella, calls himself Coulter, he still thinks it was fun. He likes to think he's some kind of bad man. But later I was talking to Miss Abigail and she said you'd just been talking with her when you was buying supplies. That fella from back east somewheres, well, he's got some strange ideas, I reckon.'

Fagan smiled. He couldn't really blame the men who'd held him. At the same time he didn't think too much of them for it either. But when the big boss told a hand to do something, well, that's all it took. 'All right, so I guess if I've got someone to be mad at, it'd be the Easterner. You were only doing what you were told.'

'That don't make it right, though.'

'I have to agree, but don't let it worry you.'

'Well, you see it does, 'cause I hear you're looking for hands and I'd like to hire on. Kind of a way to show you I ain't that bad a person, you see?'

'You're no longer working at Crown?'

'No sir. I didn't like it when I learned what'd really happened. When I told Coulter, he just laughed and, well, we got into it. Nixon stopped the fight and when Coulter told him what I'd said, Nixon fired me. I was gonna quit anyhow.'

Again Fagan hesitated. He could use another hand but hiring someone that had worked for Nixon might not be too smart. He didn't trust Nixon and if the Crown foreman was stealing Crown beef then it was certain he'd have to have the help of a few of the crew.

Bringing this man on to the Box M could be trouble.

'I'm a good rider, Mister Fagan. Henshaw, he knows me and will vouch for me.'

Thinking about it further, Fagan pursed his lips and frowned. No, from what he could see, Nixon wasn't the kind of thinker to work out an underhanded plan such as planting a man in the Box M crew. Hells bells, what harm could it do anyway? And Box M could use the man.

'What'll Nixon or the Crown crew say when they see you riding with Box M?'

'I dunno. But a man's gotta have work, don't he? Anyway, I was just another of the hands at Crown, not one of the hard men Nixon has around him. I reckon that's what Coulter wants, to be one of that gang.'

Fagan thought about it a bit more and then nodded. 'You got your horse and saddle?'

'Yes sir, right back there,' Collins

jerked a thumb over his shoulder.

'OK. We'll be riding out in a little while. You can ride along with us.'

* * *

Explaining that he'd hired another rider, Fagan nodded toward where Collins was standing, still keeping in the shadows.

'Oh, yeah, that's Sam Collins. He's been part of the Crown crew for a couple years. I've seen him at roundups before. He'll do.' Lifting a hand he gave the new man a short wave. 'Why's he keeping out of sight?'

'Nixon fired him, he says. I figure he wants to get settled in with the Box M before anyone notices. How much longer is Miss Mary Ellen going to be?'

'Oh, she's about ready. I helped her load the supplies in the back of the wagon so we can head back to the ranch any time.'

* * *

Once again, Mary Ellen didn't pay any attention to Fagan as she called her goodbyes to her friend and reined the wagon around and out of town. The three riders dropped in behind her, keeping a short ways back.

The ride along the ranch road wasn't much different from the first time Fagan had ridden it. Sam Collins, after a few brief words with Henshaw, slouched comfortably in the saddle and rode without speaking. Fagan, letting his horse drop behind the two, thought about his run-in with Nixon.

So far, all he'd heard about the Crown foreman was that the man was iron tough. Looking at it, he hadn't done very much since riding into town except getting beat up by some dude and almost getting into a fight with Nixon. Oh, he added silently, glancing ahead at the back of the wagon, and somehow irritating Miss Mary Ellen. Now there, he thought with a wide smile, was something very interesting.

Since being introduced by her father,

Fagan had yet to see anything but frowns on her face. But, he said to himself, she certainly had the makings of a good, bright smile. Her suntanned face wasn't the slender beauty of Abigail Duniway's. It was rounder, with high cheekbones causing her eyes to slant up a little at the edges. Those eyes, he remembered, were the kind of blue that was seen in a cloudless spring morning, a pale sparkling clear blue.

'Why,' he went on silently. 'I'll bet her teeth just gleam, framed by her smooth sun-browned skin.'

Letting his glance fall to the two riders ahead, he was glad no one could see the smile he felt stretching his face.

9

A short way out from the ranch, Mary Ellen snapped the whip over the head of the horse pulling the wagon, sending it into a run up toward the buildings. By the time he and the others reached the barn, the young woman had disappeared and Moses had unhitched the horse and was giving the animal a rub down.

Silas Turnbull came down to the barn after the men rode in to find out how the hiring went. The three riders were just rubbing down their mounts when the ranch owner came in.

'How'd ya do?' he asked, his face looking weary with concern. 'Mary Ellen says you brought one of Crown's hands with you.'

'She's right,' Fagan said, 'we ended up getting four others, too.'

Seeing the rancher looking Sam over,

Fagan made the introduction. 'This here is Sam Collins. He's one of the men we took on for the roundup.'

'Mister Turnbull,' Sam shook the offered hand.

'You were working for Crown, weren't you?' Turnbull asked.

'Yeah, but I had a little disagreement with Nixon and left. Mister Fagan here offered me the job, at least through the roundup.'

'Well, that's what I hired him to do. Welcome to the ranch. Now, Elias, if you've got a minute, I'd like to talk to you about that roundup. Come on up to the house.'

Fagan nodded to the men and walked with his boss across the yard. 'I gather Miss Mary Ellen got here without any trouble?'

'Yes, and I gave her gruff for running her horse like that, too. She said something about not wanting to take all day to get back to the ranch but I'm not sure it was necessary to half-kill that animal.'

'Well, you know how women can be, I reckon. After spending most of the day with her good friend, I suppose getting back to the quiet of the ranch sounded too good to put off.'

Climbing up the steps to the porch, Turnbull caught Fagan's eye. 'You don't have to cover for her, Mister Fagan.'

Fagan didn't have anything to say to that, but followed the older man into the house. Passing through the big living room, Turnbull led the way into a little room off to one side. A desk covered with paper and tally books declared this was the owner's office.

'Take a chair, there, and I'll see about a little refreshment.' Turnbull stepped back out of the room to return a moment later carrying a bottle and two glasses. 'Cognac. I bought a few bottles the last time I was down in Denver at a Cattleman's Association meeting. This is the last of it so after we get the cattle shipped I'll have to make another trip south, I reckon.'

130

Pouring the drinks, he handed one glass to Fagan and, lifting his in a toast, said, 'Happy days.'

Fagan nodded and sipping the liquor, smiled. Good French cognac wasn't to be had in every saloon and was appreciated when it was available.

'I wanted to talk to you about that man you hired, Sam Collins. Are you sure he's not a plant, someone working for Crown to keep a watch on things here at the Box M?'

'I don't think he is more than an out-of-work cowboy,' Fagan thought a moment and then decided to tell Turnbull how they had first met. 'He was one of the two men who held me when that tenderfoot, Peeters, took it upon himself to teach me a lesson. Sam says they had been led to believe that I had bad-mouthed Miss Abigail Duniway and when he found out the truth, raised a bit of a stink over it. Nixon fired him on the spot.'

'Ah, well. There's a lot of grief that's come because of that fight. I can't figure it out, but somehow that's what Mary Ellen is holding against you, too. I'll tell you the truth, I never understood her mother and I'll never understand her. I've my doubts that she'll ever learn to think like an adult has to.'

Fagan took a sip of his drink so to hide his smile and not have to say anything.

'But that's not what I wanted to talk about. The men you hired should fill out the crew pretty well.'

'Yes. The blacksmith, Marchal, said he'd keep an eye out for any more if you think we'll need more. Those four will be riding in early in the morning.'

'Good, good. That'll make it a lot easier. What has to be done is to begin the job of chasing the stock out of the ravines and gullies. We call all that broken land that fronts up to the steep bluff from the farthest edge of the badlands north the breaks. It's all brush-choked country and the stupid critters like to winter back in there. I guess 'cause it's protected from winter storms. Anyway, that's where most of the new stuff'll be hiding. Rough, dangerous working back in there, too, so make sure everyone rides carefully.'

'I've worked country like that before. What'll be best is to put one of the new hands with someone who knows the area. Have a couple more pushing the critters on toward the holding ground, keeping them from turning around.'

'Yeah, sounds like you know what you're doing. All right, I'll be sending the cook wagon out in a few days. Early on you and the crew'll be close enough to come in come evening but it won't be long before you'll be too far out. We've got the back corral filled with horses so there'll be enough for the men. I had Crauley over on the B-slash-B shoe up a couple dozen head. I don't know how he does it, but since he came into the basin we've always had enough riding stock. So there you go. Keep me informed as things develop.'

Finishing his drink, Fagan got out of the chair and nodding his good night, left the older man sitting behind his desk.

Hoping he might see Mary Ellen, he took his time leaving the house, but she was nowhere in sight.

★ ★ ★

The extra riders were waiting by the corral fence when Fagan and the others poured out of the bunkhouse the next morning. The eastern sky was just beginning to show light and the heavy blanket of stars could still be seen overhead.

'Morning' boys,' the new foreman called. 'You're just in time for breakfast.' Waving a hand, he led the way to the cook shack.

After a heavy meal of flapjacks with lots of honey, bacon, eggs, hash browns, biscuits and gravy, he sent the men out in two-man teams to start the work of moving cattle. Most of the new men had worked on the Box M in other years and were familiar with the country. Not overly familiar with the gullies and ravines that backed up to the bluffs, he had Sam ride out with him, figuring to take the farthest section to begin with.

'There's a lot I don't know about Crown,' he said as the two men rode side by side to the mouth of a narrow valley. Pulling up, they sat for a moment rolling a smoke and studying the draw. At some time in the far distant past, water had washed down from the steep cliff face, leaving behind a mile-long defile that rose as it narrowed. Manzanita, the smooth red bark contrasting with the shiny green foliage, made the way look impassible.

'This isn't going to be any fun at all,' said Fagan. 'They tell me not to be surprised if we come up with a lot of mama cows missing their young'uns. Henshaw seems to think the final tally won't be as good as last year's was and last winter wasn't so bad as to account for it. Do you think the same thing has happened over at Crown?'

'Boy,' Sam grimaced, 'this is one part of the job I purely hate. Darn glad I'm wearing my oldest pair of jeans. The branches of that scrub brush will tear right through a pair of pants in a hurry.' Taking a deep drag of his cigarette, he glanced at Fagan. 'Look, Mister Fagan, I appreciate the work, especially after everything I helped do to you. But it just wouldn't be decent of me to tell tales about Nixon or the way Crown does business. You understand?'

Fagan smiled. 'Yeah, I do. And I respect your honesty. But a man hires on and from that moment on, he rides for the brand. Even now.'

Sam sighed and pinched out the butt. 'Yeah. I just feel like a kid carrying tales if I go to talking about Nixon and Crown.'

'All right. I won't ask any more questions. As long as it doesn't hurt the Box M, I suppose it isn't any of my business, is it? Well, this isn't getting any cattle outa there.' Poking a heel into the side of his mount, he started the animal forward.

For the next couple hours the two men rode slowly through the brush, keeping some distance between them. Cattle, pushed by the riders, bolted out of the shade they'd been lying in only to disappear further along. As the walls of the ravine started to close, the half-wild critters found they had no place to go and turned back between the riders. When he and Sam reached the end of the draw they turned their horses around and rode back out, pushing cattle ahead of them.

Once out of the confines of the ravine, the cattle, mostly two-year-old heifers with a few bulls mixed in, settled down to chomping at the new spring grasses. Taking a rough count, Fagan saw few yearlings. Riding back and forth, the riders kept pushing the small herd until it was some distance from the mouth of the ravine.

'That's probably enough,' Fagan

called, reining in. Other hands, doing the same thing, would, as they rode along to the next shallow gully, drive the cattle a little more. As the work progressed, the small jags of beef would be pushed closer and closer to the holding grounds. That's where the real work of branding and separating the stock slated for market would take place.

Fagan and Sam had just reached the top end of a second ravine and were starting back, when movement up on the top of the ravine wall caught the foreman's eye. Turning in the saddle, he saw the afternoon sun flash off something metal at the same instant he heard the boom of a rifle. Without thinking, he dove out of the saddle landing on a shoulder and rolling behind the cover of a bush.

10

'Hey,' he heard Sam call, 'what's going on over there.'

Fagan, his Colt drawn and the hammer thumbed back, didn't respond but lay still, watching where the shot had come from.

For a long minute there was nothing and then Sam rode up leading Fagan's horse by the reins. 'What the hell, you got somebody mad at you?'

'That's the second time in a handful of days someone has tried to dry-gulch me and I don't know why,' Fagan said, keeping the horses between him and that side of the ravine. 'He was up there. I saw a flash of sunlight on something and ducked.'

'Good thing you did, look,' Sam was pointing at the bullet scar cutting Fagan's saddle. 'Whoever's after you got too close that time.'

'Yeah,' Fagan felt his legs shake and leaned against the horse's chest.

'What're you gonna do? Sooner or later you ain't gonna be so damn lucky and he'll get you.'

For a long moment Fagan stood still, letting his body settle down.

'What would you have done, saying the shooter had hit me?'

'What? Well, do what I could to patch you up, less'n you was dead. Then I guess I'd see if I could find out who it was before taking your body back to the ranch. Why?'

'Let's say you and I were a bit apart and you heard the shot. You came rushing over to find out what'd happened just in time to see me, all bent over my saddle, riding a spooked horse hell bent for leather in that direction.' He pointed on across the other way, toward the lowest part of the ravine wall away from where the shooter had been.

'Why would you do that?'

'You said it, sooner or later he'll get a

good shot and I'll be dead. So, if everybody thinks this time I was hit, it'd give me time to look around. There's got to be a reason for this, I just don't know what it is. If I had a few days, out of sight and alone, I might be able to find out who's riding where they shouldn't be.'

'Hell, if'n I rode back to the ranch to tell that whopper every hand on the place'd be out searching for you, or what's left of you.'

'Yeah, for a day or two. But the roundup's got to go on. If everybody thought I'd been shot then they would expect my horse or my body to show up sometime. So, all I have to do is stay out of sight while the search is going on. Once the men have gone back to the roundup I can start my search.'

'What're you gonna live on during that time? There ain't much forage out here, unless you skin out a beef or something.'

Fagan looked out over the range. 'That is one thing . . . well, how about after a day or two, say two days, you squirrel away some grub from the cook shack. Cookie'll be bringing the chuck wagon out about then and you can raid the kitchen pantry. The men'll be back working the cattle and you can get away, bring me a loaded pair of saddle-bags. Drop them here and go back. Don't say anything to anyone, just do your job and I'll be doing mine.'

'I dunno, Mister Fagan. It don't sound too good to me.'

'What do you want, that I should ignore the fact that someone has tried twice to blow my head off?'

Sam chuckled. 'It weren't your head that'd be blown off if that bullet had hit you,' he said, touching the gouge in the saddle leather. 'Well, I guess you know what you're doing. All right, I'll do what you say.'

'Good. Now, empty out those sandwiches you're carrying and I'll run this horse out of here. That way when anyone comes looking, they'll find the tracks. If you play your part right and I stay hid, it'll all work out.'

★ ★ ★

Everything worked like he'd planned, at least for a while. Patting the horse he'd been riding, a young brown-colored mustang, a couple times on the neck as Sam sat in his saddle and watched, Fagan smiled.

'I do hope this horse can forgive me. See you in a few days, Sam, and thanks.'

Before the young cowboy could respond, Fagan had jammed his spurs into the animal's flanks and was almost unseated when the horse took off. Not breaking stride, the mustang ran full out, swerving one way and then another around the sharp branches of low-lying brush. Climbing up the side of the ravine and wide-eyed with fright, the horse's hooves barely touched the ground as it fled the monster that had bitten it in the sides. Rushing down the other side, Fagan nearly pulled back on the reins when he saw a drop-off dead ahead, but didn't. Any sign he left would have to look natural for a panicked horse.

The drop-off turned out to be only the sharp edge of a ditch formed by last winter's run off and the mustang jumped it, not slowing at all. Straightaway it ran until, his brown hide covered with thick foam, it started to falter. Reining back toward the broken ground of the bluff, Fagan let the horse slow to an uneven trot and then continuing on in a shambling walk. When he saw a large open piece of ground ahead, he urged his mount that way.

Once on a stretch of hardpan he pulled the horse to a stop and swung down, standing for a moment while he looked back the way he had come. Sam and the little clearing in the ravine he'd been in were out of sight in the undulating landscape.

The tough little mustang stood

unmoving for a long time, its sides heaving. Slowly, as the horse's breathing came more regular, Fagan started leading it away, at right angles to the piece of rock-hard earth. Stopping after a short distance, the mustang stood with its head down, unmoving as the rider used a leafy branch from a bush to carefully sweep all traces of his passage away. It wouldn't fool an Indian tracker, he thought looking over his handiwork, but it'd do.

Still leading the horse, he walked further on, keeping to the edge of the steep bluffs that limited movement in that direction. Just as the sun was dropping behind the bluff overhead he found what he was searching for, a small spring in a shady little pocket of stunted pine trees.

Stripping the saddle from the tired mustang, Fagan watched as the animal first drank from the little pool that collected the water before rolling in the sandy dirt beyond. This, he decided, would do as a hiding place while the search for his body went on. A patch of grass would keep his horse nearby and he had the sandwiches he and Sam had been carrying. The only thing missing, he thought, was his bedroll. Using the sweaty saddle blanket might fight off the early morning cold air, but he didn't think he could get past the strong horse smell.

Sleep that night was broken, first by the hundreds of little rocks that poked him no matter which way he lay and later by the chill that settled into the little pocket. Sitting with his back against the shredded bark-covered trunk of a pine, he wrapped his arms tightly around his chest, trying to keep from shivering. The cold, as well as not having a cup of morning coffee to look forward to, made the morning a long time coming.

All through the day, as the mustang rested and fed on the young, tender grass, Fagan nibbled at the sandwiches, never taking enough to satisfy his empty stomach, but unwilling to gobble them down. Figuring the search was on in full swing, he stayed close to the spring, not wanting to even climb higher to see what was happening. It gave him a lot of time to think about the two ambushes and who the shooter could have been. It also gave him a lot of time to think of hot coffee and a meal of bacon and eggs.

Late that afternoon he took his time to pour cut tobacco into a creased bit of paper, making the exercise last as long as possible. He went to bed, such as it was, that night after a meal of cold spring water. His horse, having fed throughout the day, stood comfortably on three legs, head hanging as it dozed.

★   ★   ★

The sun traveled across the sky on the second day like it had hobbles on, taking forever to reach its zenith. Finally, with his stomach growling, he saddled up and, taking a more round-about approach to the ravine he'd left

Sam in, rode back.

Coming from up near the blank face of the bluff he circled around and found where his attacker had crouched when taking aim. The empty brass casing, scuff marks left by the toe of a boot and a round indention where the shooter had placed a knee were the only signs. The empty was from a .44 caliber rifle, likely the most common rifle on the range.

Standing at the place and looking down, he watched as Sam came slowly riding up the shallow canyon. From where he stood, Fagan couldn't see anyone following the young rider. Dropping back to where he'd tied his horse, he was starting to swing into the saddle when he saw a thin piece of metal sticking out of the sand. Picking it up, he saw it was about half of a well-worn iron horseshoe. From the lack of rust, it didn't look like it'd been laying there long.

Sitting the saddle, he thought about it. Finding where a rider's horse had thrown a shoe wouldn't be out of the ordinary in most places, but not here. Shoving the shoe into a saddle-bag, he rode down to meet up with Sam.

★　★　★

'We had the entire crew out searching for you,' Sam said, tossing a pair of fully packed saddle-bags to Fagan before ground hitching his horse. 'Followed your trail until it was lost and then spread out and beat the brush until dark. Damn, it was as hard work as chasing cows outa the scrub.'

Fagan, busy building a small fire, laughed. 'Didn't find me, though, did you.'

Sam smiled and shook his head. 'Nope. Turnbull was on everybody's tail, too. He wanted to send the hands out the next day but Henshaw argued against it. Said it was better to go on with the roundup. Your body'd probably show up like Caldwell's did, he said. That didn't make the old man very happy, I'll tell you.'

'I wouldn't be surprised if we failed to fool Henshaw,' Fagan said as he emptied a canteen of water into a fire-blackened coffee pot and dropped in a handful of crushed beans. Even before getting into the sack of grub that Sam had brought, he was going to have his coffee. 'Not much gets by that old man.'

'Well, it sure sounds like someone does have it in for the Box M bosses. Darn sure I wouldn't want that job. Wonder what it's all about?'

Another rider, leading a horse, stepped out from behind the thick brush. 'Yes, I can hardly wait to hear what this is all about, myself.'

11

'What exactly are you up to, Mister Foreman,' Mary Ellen Turnbull said, her eyes boring into Fagan's. 'Let's hear your reason for disappearing.'

'Ah, Miss Mary Ellen,' Sam started to say, stopping when the young woman raised a hand.

'You'll have your chance to talk in a minute. First I want to hear what this man has to say. And I want the truth.'

After getting over his initial surprise, Fagan had hunkered back down and pushed another stick into the fire.

'Sam,' he said, ignoring the woman's question, 'you worked the Crown herd so you'd know. Honest now, do you think they're missing stock?'

'Huh?' the cowboy looked first at Mary Ellen and then at the foreman. Stubbing a toe in the dirt and studying the result so he wouldn't have to look at

Fagan directly, he hesitated before going on. 'Well, yeah. There aren't as much young stuff showing up as you'd figure and . . . well, I reckon there'll be a smaller herd to ship this year. Yeah.'

Fagan nodded and continued to watch the steam start to rise from the coffee pot. 'I guess what everyone's saying about cattle being rustled is true, wouldn't you say?'

'Oh, yeah, I guess. Look, Mister Fagan, I don't know how it's done but, yeah there's been stock missing from Crown for a couple years. Least there hasn't been as many head as everyone that's been on the place for more'n two or three years think there should be. All I know for sure is the first year I was working over there it took us better'n a week to do the branding. As I recall, it took closer to twice that long. The next year was some quicker and last year, well, we were done in five or six days.'

'Dad thinks we've been missing cattle too. But so far it's only talk. And then you show up. What is this all about,' Mary Ellen demanded, stomping a foot.

Lifting the pot off the fire, Fagan looked up at her. 'Did you bring a cup?'

Frowning, she shook her head.

'Sam, you got a cup you could lend her?'

Puzzled, the rider dug in a saddle-bag and handed her a tin cup.

'OK then,' Fagan said, pouring the coffee and then looking up at Sam, 'you head on back to the roundup and Miss Mary Ellen and I'll have a little talk. Remember, not a word to anyone. Far as it goes, I'm still lying out there somewhere, dead as a Christmas goose.'

Not understanding, Sam hesitated for a minute before, with a last shake of his head, he swung into the saddle and, not looking back, rode away.

'Now then, young lady, if you'd be so kind as to pull up a chair we'll have our little talk.'

'Go ahead, make jokes if you want,

but I demand to know what you're up to.'

Fagan smiled and held out a cup. 'Be careful, that's plenty hot.'

He waited until she gave up and took the cup, sat down on the ground, being careful to keep on the other side of the small fire from him.

'OK. I'm listening.'

'You know a fella named Frank Goodall?'

The question surprised her. 'Well, yes. He's the marshal down in Golden. He's the one Father telegraphed about our cattle being rustled. What's he got to do with anything?'

'Federal Marshal Frank Goodall,' Fagan emphasized the full title, 'asked me, seeing as I was pretty footloose at the time, if I'd come up to Short Creek to look into that report of rustling. So, here I am. I explained all this to your pa and that's why he hired me to fill in as foreman, to give me a chance to look around.'

The young woman frowned. 'Why

would a federal marshal ask you to do his job?'

Fagan sipped the hot brew and nearly sighed with pleasure. 'Well, he knew I'd carried a badge up in Wyoming and that I know a little about cattle. He's got his hands full down in Golden with some holdups and couldn't find time to come himself.'

Mary Ellen, still frowning, studied the ground, thinking.

'Now,' said Fagan after a moment, 'you can tell me, why did you take such a quick dislike to me? From the get-go you were looking daggers whenever I was close by. I'm not that ugly, am I?'

'Do you have to make light of everything?' she exclaimed, then settled back. 'It's because of my friend, Abigail Duniway. Abby is my best friend and she wants to marry Mister Peeters.'

'So, what's that got to do with me?'

'You rode into town and wormed your way between them. I want her to have what she wants and that isn't some common drifter, even if you are a friend of a federal marshal.' Anger cut through her words, making them hard.

Fagan chuckled. 'Whoooie. Now that's something. I stop for supplies and flirt a little with a young woman and end up getting beat on. And then on top of that, earn the extreme dislike of the boss's daughter.'

'It isn't funny. I heard what Mister Peeters did and I don't condone it one bit, but I also heard the way Abby talked about you. She's my best friend and has been since we first came into this part of the country. Fact is, she's about the only other girl this side of Golden. Look,' she hesitated a bit then, glancing down, shook her head side to side, 'maybe I've been rude and, well, overly protective of her and if so, then I apologize. But, well, she's my friend.'

'And you're afraid I'm going to cause trouble for her? You must not think much of their romance.'

Mary Ellen grimaced. 'I won't say anything against her, but, yes, there are times when I think she's after that fella from back east just because he's rich.'

'Oh, I get it. You're afraid I'll bewitch your best friend and make her forget her plans to snare the rich greenhorn, plans you really don't approve of?'

Mary Ellen paused and then, still not looking up, shook her head back and forth. 'No. Well, I mean . . . what I mean is that I don't want anyone causing Abby any problems. But,' she sat up straight, changing the subject abruptly, 'that's not explaining why that rider was bringing you food? How did you get him to do that, anyway?'

'Probably because he'd been close by when someone tried to shoot me. The idea is simple. I've been shot at from ambush twice since leaving Golden. If everybody thinks I'm dead then that someone will stop trying to surprise me and if I'm not tied to the roundup I can take time to look around. Look for evidence of who's doing the rustling as well as who shot Caldwell and has tried to kill me.'

'Why, do you think Caldwell's death

is tied in with the rustling? I don't see that. He worked for us long before we came on to this range. For at least ten years, since I was a little girl. He wouldn't have had anything to do with stealing from the ranch.'

'How was it your father decided to build his operation here?'

Fagan was taken aback to see her shoulders soften. 'We had a good-sized spread down on the Texas panhandle and things were good until Mother took sick and just couldn't seem to get any better. It worried Pa and he lost interest in everything. He took her to a special kind of doctor up in Abilene but she came home as sick as she was when they had got on the train. Anyway, our ranch foreman, Karl Caldwell, had been on the place for as long as I could remember and he tried to keep things going. Most of the hands did what they could, but without Pa showing any concern, things just seemed to down hill. Then we had a damaging winter and the next spring there wasn't enough rain, and even with Karl's help it wasn't long before there was trouble getting enough cattle to sell. When a loan with the bank came due there wasn't much we could do. Dad didn't seem to care one way or another until someone said that maybe a change might do Mother some good. Pa sold everything, hoping things might improve and for a time it did. We had to start over again and start a lot smaller. We ended up here and for a while Mother got better and Pa was back to running the ranch. But that didn't last long. Mother just didn't wake up one morning. That was three years ago and just recently has Pa gotten over it. Anyway, here we are and the Box M is doing well. Dad is almost his old self again and the place is on firm footing financially. No bank loans or anything. But then last year, just like that cowhand said, we didn't have as many head to sell as we should have. Karl did a rough range tally and thinks, um, thought, we'd lost even more this last

159

winter. Now, Dad is starting to act funny again.'

Slowly as she talked, her voice had become softer and more worried sounding.

There was still one thing that didn't make sense to Fagan. 'And then your foreman, Karl Caldwell, disappeared. Didn't you think that was funny? I mean after helping out for so long as he did?'

'No, not really. Karl was a great help but he'd talked about wanting to go back to Texas before. He had some relations back there and, well, when he didn't come back after a Saturday in town we thought he'd just decided to ride on. Do you really think he was killed by rustlers?'

'From the bullet hole in the back of his shirt, I think it's likely. It's possible he saw something he shouldn't have and had to be killed to keep it a secret. I don't know, but if I'm out there chasing cows and ducking bullets I won't be able to find out, now will I.'

'So you want to stay dead for a while.'

'Yep, that's the plan. What are you going to do to help me out?'

'I still don't think much of you but if you're dead then you won't be messing up Abigail's dreams, will you.'

Fagan laughed. 'Lady, you can put that idea away somewhere. Your best friend is not my idea of a partner to take to a wedding.'

'Oh, and why not? She's beautiful and her father's quite well off. I think she'd be a good catch for someone like you.'

'Nope. In the first place, someone like me doesn't need or want her pa's money or position. Certainly, the mother of my children won't be a city girl. The woman I ask to spend the rest of my life with and help raise our children has to be comfortable with horses, cattle and ranch life.' He paused and wearing a slight smile took time to look her over. 'Someone more like you, I'd say.'

Flustered, Mary Ellen tossed the coffee dregs from her cup as she got to her feet. Dropping the cup next to the saddle-bags Sam had left, she stepped to her horse.

'All right,' anger was back in her words, 'I can understand what you're doing. I won't say anything to anyone, but don't look for any more help from me.'

'There you go again, mad at me for no reason. Ah, well, nobody said it'd be easy.'

Climbing into the saddle, the young woman spoke over her shoulder as she reined the horse away. 'I don't know what you mean. And I certainly don't care, either.'

Touching a heel to her mount, she headed back the way she'd come, disappearing into the brush. Fagan laughed softly and, after drinking the last of his coffee, picked up the saddle-bags and headed for his horse. If she could find him then the man who was trying to shoot him might. It was time to go play dead again.

12

For the next week, riding in ever widening circles, always careful to stay away from the cowboys working at making the gather, Fagan rode the Box M range. More than once, after finding a few head that had been missed, he spent some time moving them in the direction of the holding grounds. But except for that, by the time the food Sam Collins had brought him was nearly gone, he hadn't found anything out of place. On the bright side, he said to himself one morning as he boiled water for coffee, the last of the beans in the saddle-bags, in that time nobody had taken a shot at him.

After finishing his meal, he settled back to think about what to do next. Nearly out of food, and now out of coffee, the only thing he could see to do was give it up.

Comfortable and safely hidden in the willows and cottonwood trees that grew thickly on the Box M side of the Blue River overlooking the ford that Henshaw had talked of, he looked out across the shallows, seeing only more brush and trees on the other side. That would be Crown land, he thought, wondering if it'd do any good to take a ride over that way.

Thinking about it, he decided it wouldn't tell him anything. Hard to tell what brand a critter's carrying by looking at hoof prints in the dirt, and there'd certainly be a lot of that most everywhere on Crown land. If someone was taking stock from the two ranches and running them to a buyer at the railhead, then that someone would have to be coming across the river, making a little gather of Box M stock and herding them across the ford. Mixing as many head wearing Crown's brand as a few men could handle and driving them south to Golden, all the time not letting any of the Crown hands get wind of it would be hard. Darn near impossible. Even as big as Crown was, any sign of cattle being moved would be quickly spotted.

And why, he asked himself, would they want to mix some of the Box M's longhorn Durham mix in with Crown's longhorns anyway? The distinctive bigger shouldered Durham breed would stand out like an Arabian in a herd of mustangs. Then there was the fact that the heavier beef wouldn't trail as fast as longhorns. No self-respecting rustler would want that kind of hindrance, not if a long drive to get to a buyer was to be made.

No, he sat back frowning, there were too many unanswered questions to this whole thing.

Finishing the coffee, he made sure his little fire was out and, after tightening the mustang's cinches, sat in the saddle for a minute, waiting for inspiration.

Looking far ahead, toward the east, he could see how the land began its long climb up toward the Moguls.

From where he sat he could make out a faint wagon road that came from the pass, heading into Short Creek itself. Any stolen Box M cattle being moved south would have to be brought across the river here and that would be dangerous. This ford was too out in the open. Of course, if a couple riders pushed a small jag over there and let them graze until late in the night, before pushing them across the river, come daylight they'd be gone. Working at night and keeping it quiet it might work. Once the cattle were mixed with some Crown stock anybody would have to ride close to see the brands. It could be done that way.

Movement along the road caught his eye and he backed the horse deeper into the trees as a ranch wagon turned off the road and headed for the ford. That, Fagan thought, would be a Crown wagon. Probably some Crown hand checking out how things were progressing at the holding ground at Big Flats. Climbing out of the saddle, he held his hand over the mustang's nose to keep it from making any noise as the team slowed as it reached the water.

The wagon was halfway across the river when Fagan recognized the horses. It was the matched team of bays that had been pulling the Easterner's wagon the day he'd first ridden into town. Handling the reins was, he saw, the tenderfoot himself. And he was alone.

Smiling, Fagan waited until the wagon was almost across before swinging into the saddle and, kneeing the mustang forward, rode up just as the wagon started up the Crown bank.

'Now, will you look here,' Fagan pulled up at the head of the off horse. 'If it isn't my good friend, Mister Tenderfoot Peeters.'

'Who . . . who in blazes are you? Get out of my way. You're trespassing on my land. Get away from me.'

'Oh, no sir, I can't do that. Not this time,' Fagan swung down and tied his horse's reins to the headstall of one of the bays. 'And as far as who I am, if you think back a while, you'll remember.'

Peeters, alarmed, stood up, reaching for the thin whip sitting in a socket next to the wagon's dash. 'What do you think you're doing? Untie that horse and get out of my way, I tell you.'

'Nope,' Fagan couldn't stop smiling. Unbuckling his gunbelt, he hooked it over his saddle horn and walked over to stand next to the wagon.

'Think back to when you had two of your hired hands hold me while you beat on me. Oh, that hurt, it did. Busted a rib or two, according to the doctor. But that's all better now and here you are, all alone with no hired hands to help hold me.'

'Yes, I do remember you. You're the drifter that was getting fresh with Miss Abigail. Yes, you're the one. Well, if you want more of what I gave you, I'll certain oblige you.'

Climbing down from the wagon, Peeters tugged at his driving gloves.

'But in all fairness, I must warn you. I learned the fine art of fisticuffs from experts. Although I doubt you know what that means. Well,' putting his curled fists up, his left near his chin and his right out in front, 'I will be more than happy to give you a lesson.'

Bouncing on his toes a couple times, Peeters moved around a little, dancing away from the wagon. Fagan watched, his hands hanging at his sides. The smile didn't waver when, still springing on his toes, Peeters charged forward lashing out with his right fist. Fagan ducked to one side a little before bringing a knotted fist up, slamming it into the man's ribcage.

The blow stopped Peeters's attack and for a second he dropped his hands. Not wasting any time, Fagan stepped in and, bringing another fist up from the ground, connected with the man's chin. Peeters fell back, landing flat on his back.

'I say,' said Peeters, rubbing his chin, 'that blow wasn't exactly fair.'

'Come on, get up and I'll show you more of what's not exactly fair.'

'Um, no, I think not. You win your battle. If I stay down, you can't very well continue, can you. If I get up, I fear you'll hurt me. And it is clear; you are out to hurt me.'

'You're damn tooting, I am. Get up and show me some more of your lessons.'

Wincing as he moved, and using his hands and feet, Peeters crawled back until he was seated with his back against a wagon wheel. 'No, I know when I've lost. To tell the truth, I never was much of a fighter. And I'll add to that. I wasn't very proud of myself for the way I treated you in town. It was all because of the way Miss Abigail looked at you in the store that day, you know. I am not sure she ever looks at me that way. It made me, well, I guess you could say, it made me a little crazy.'

'So I'm supposed to just forget it? You are a foreigner to the west, aren't you? I'll tell you, it's a good thing I'm a nice guy or I'd stop talking to you and simply pistol whip you.'

'Yes, I can see how a person could do that. Another case of the beating making you a little crazy, I would say. Well, I can't stop you.'

'Ah, the hell with it,' Fagan grouched.

'You know, my father sent me out here to the Wild West in the hopes that it would make a man of me. Impossible, I'd say, to make a diamond out of a piece of clay. I imagine he did what he thought was best, however. The only good outcome is that I met Miss Abigail. Now all I want to do is go home, taking her with me, of course. Dear Father would not approve of that, I dare say.'

'Dammit, I don't want to hear about your troubles, I've enough of my own.' Fagan snarled, wrapping his gunbelt back around his waist. 'If you want to go back to old New York, then go. Don't just sit there in the dirt and bawl about it. Get up and go. You can certainly afford the ticket, can't you?'

'Oh, of course I can. But you see, I couldn't return east until Father tells me to and I won't leave without Miss Abigail. And she has not yet agreed to my proposal.'

'Ah, well, forget it.' Putting a foot in a stirrup, Fagan climbed aboard. 'You are something else, I'll say that. Damn fool, is what you are.' Reining around, he headed back into the trees. Out of sight, he hauled up and thought.

'Talk about being a fool,' he said to the mustang. 'Riding away isn't going to help me at all.'

Turning back, he watched as Peeters stood, and after brushing off his pants, climbed back on to the wagon seat. Snapping the whip over the heads of the horses, and sitting with his shoulders all hunched over, he rode away.

'Damn fool,' Fagan repeated himself.

13

Crossing back on to Box M land, he sat slouched in the saddle, letting the mustang set its own pace as he thought about what little he'd found since the ambush. Shaking his head in disgust, he touched a booted heel to the horse's flank. Maybe, he said to himself, it was time for a meal at the hotel.

Full dark had come on by the time he reached the bridge at the northern end of Short Creek's main street. Lanterns lighting a few of the shop windows indicated some businesses were still open. The double doors of the blacksmith shop were one of these. Marchal's forge was a bright yellow beacon in the evening's darkness.

'Hey, there, Mister Blacksmith, you got time to shoe up a horse?' he called out softly before swinging down. Having been in the saddle all day for the past couple of weeks, Fagan stood for a moment feeling the stiffness in his legs.

'No, dammit, not tonight,' Marchal snarled. 'Don't you cowboys think I got a life of my own? What're ya thinking about, coming in this late and expecting I'll jump — ' Peering at the rider standing by his horse, the smithy squinted his eyes to better see who he was talking to. 'What the hell — ?'

'Evening, Eloy,' Fagan smiled and stepped closer to the light of the forge.

'Well, hells fire. Elias Fagan. Man, you're supposed to be dead. What're you doing coming around here all alive and in one piece?'

'Nope, I'm not dead and my horse doesn't need shoeing either. Just on my way over to the hotel restaurant for a meal and thought I'd see if you'd had supper yet.'

Striding out, Marchal grabbed Fagan's hand. 'Well, am I glad to see you. Everybody said you'd been shot in the back and your horse ran off and . . . Wait a minute, what's this all about?'

Fagan laughed. 'C'mon. Close those doors and let's go see about food. I'll tell you all about it over a cup of good coffee. All I've had has been campfire coffee and I ran out of that. Come on. I'll buy.'

★ ★ ★

A half-dozen or so customers were in the restaurant when Fagan and Marchal pushed through the door. Everyone stopped to stare but the two men simply ignored them and took a table against the back wall.

'All right, now, we're sitting here and I'm waiting. Tell me what the hell's going on.'

While eating the meal, Fagan, keeping his voice low, explained what he'd done, faking his death and hiding out.

'It's about the only thing I could think of to do. Whoever had taken such a big dislike to me wasn't going to miss his shot forever.'

175

'Well, did you come up with anything? Do you know who that shooter was?'

'No, I'm no closer to that than I was before.'

'Aghh, yeah,' Marchal grimaced. 'I'll bet you a plugged nickel it was someone from Crown. Either Nixon or that crazy easterner.'

'You know, every time someone says anything about rustling or back shooting, it's laid at Crown's door. Well, except when the finger is pointed at Turnbull. Somehow I don't think so. There's something else going on around here. I just haven't figured it all out yet.'

Out on the street again, the pair stopped to roll a smoke before walking back to the blacksmith shop.

'What say we stop for a quick drink,' Marchal asked, 'kinda help settle the meal, you know.'

'Not tonight, Eloy. I think I'll head on out to the Box M and have a talk with Mister Turnbull. The roundup's still going on and, after all, I was hired as foreman.'

'I gotta say, I'm feeling better, seeing as how you ain't as dead as everyone said you was.'

'Anyone in particular showing happiness at my demise?'

The blacksmith burst out laughing. 'Nope, no one in particular, I was just joshing you.'

'Well,' Fagan said taking the worn horseshoe from a saddle-bag, 'while you're in such good humor, tell me what you can about this.'

Turning serious, Marchal took the shoe and after looking at it a moment, nodded toward his shop.

'Too dark out here to really see anything,' he muttered.

Fagan followed the smithy into his office and waited until he'd lit a lantern.

'I found this up in a place no rider had any business being,' he explained. 'Is it one of yours?'

Marchal took it and, holding it in the

light, shook his head. 'No, not the kind I use. I make my shoes from stock iron. This'n is one of those machine-made shoes. They're made back east somewhere and you can buy them by the dozen. A lot of ranchers do that, put in a couple hundred shoes and then let one of the hands do the job of nailing them on as needed. It doesn't always do the best job, unless the hand knows how to do it right. But if you can't get into town all that often, its better'n not putting something on the animal's feet.'

'Any idea if this came from one of the ranches around here?'

'No,' he dragged out the word, turning the iron shoe in his hands. 'But it's been well used. More'n half the shoe's worn away. Let's see, Nixon used to have a man who was a pretty good farrier but he quit a couple years ago. Out your way, old man Moses knows a bit about shoeing a horse. Turnbull's got a small forge and they do a lot of their own work. He gets his shoes from me, though.' Looking up with a smile he went on, 'and that leaves Crauley out at the B-slash-B. With all the horse stock he's got out there, he does nearly all his own shoeing. And he don't buy anything from me, either. I'll bet that's where this came from, one of his horses.'

'Hmm,' Fagan took back the shoe and, after thinking about it a bit, tossed it into a pile of iron bits and pieces taking up a corner of the smithy. 'Now that helps a little. I guess.' Pausing he frowned, still deep in thought. 'And his place is on down south, you said?'

'Well, yeah. Actually his fences are back off there,' the blacksmith pointed westward, 'a quarter mile or so other side of town. He uses two strands of barbed wire. It runs along the town limits and then down to the river a ways before cutting back toward the badlands. The top end of his spread is that creek that runs between his land and Turnbull's outfit. His ranch buildings and corrals are all over closer to that rough country, just down a piece from the creek, as I recall. Ain't been out there since he took over the land, though. He could have changed things around some, I suppose.'

'You said Crown was here and then Turnbull came in and bought up the Box M? When did Crauley buy his place?'

'Oh, it was just recent. Say two years ago? Yeah. Maybe three. Not long, though. He's done pretty good, breeding and rough breaking mustangs and he's got a bunch of fine stock, mostly Arabians. The mustangs he mostly sells to Crown and the Arabs he drives down to the railhead.'

'Well, I guess it makes some kind of sense. Silas did say he'd brought a herd of horses from the B-slash-B when we started chasing stock out of the breaks. Anyway, it's late and it's time to be heading to the bunkhouse. I've been sleeping out far too long.'

* * *

It was well past midnight when, after stripping the gear from the mustang and giving the animal a long overdue rub down, Fagan crept into the bunk house and slipped into his bed. He didn't see Henshaw lift his head and watch him tiptoe by. Smiling a little, the older man lay back down and went back to sleep.

Fagan was bombarded with questions from most of the men the next morning. Holding up a hand, he told everyone he'd explain at breakfast.

After taking time for a quick bucket bath and putting on clean clothes, his last clean shirt he noticed, he walked up to the main house. Stepping up on the porch, he was surprised when the front door opened before he could knock.

'Good morning, mister back-from-the-dead-foreman,' Mary Ellen said with a smile. Fagan noticed how the smile lit up her whole face, just, he thought, as her frown had made everything about her look dark and cold. Funny how women can do that, he said to himself as he followed her into the front room.

'And a good morning to you, Miss Mary Ellen. I'd guess that I'm no longer the top of your enemy list?' Before she could respond he went on, 'I'd like a word with your father, if he's up and around.'

'Of course I'm up,' Silas Turnbull came hurrying across to take Fagan's hand. 'What did you think, while you're out lollygagging around the country none of the rest of us would be hard at work?'

Glancing at the young woman, Fagan smiled. 'Somehow I get the idea that our little secret was shared around a bit.'

'Well, certainly,' said Mary Ellen scowled, looking first at her father then back at Fagan, 'I had to tell Father. It wouldn't be fair not to.'

'And Henshaw? I noticed he didn't seem surprised to see me this morning.'

'Yes, and Henshaw, but he didn't seem surprised. But I didn't tell anybody else, honest.'

Both men chuckled. 'All right, Elias, tell us, what did you find.'

Fagan pursed his lips a moment and then shook his head. 'Not much, I'm afraid.'

14

'Mary Ellen was a mite put out when you told her you were working with the federal marshal,' said Turnbull, motioning toward the lumpy looking sofa facing the stone fireplace. Mary Ellen quickly sat down in a wooden rocker and, hearing her father, blushed.

'Father, that isn't exactly true. I just, well, it seemed unlikely, that's all.'

Fagan tried to hide his smile as he settled back on the sofa, raising a small cloud of dust.

Turnbull chuckled. 'Guess we don't use this room much. But I wanted to have this little talk before going out to the kitchen.'

'Yeah, it won't do any good for the hands to be knowing what I'm doing here. Let them go on wondering.'

'Well, that's OK, but what are your plans now?'

Fagan shook his head. 'I've been all over your range and didn't find much. Do you have any idea how many head you're missing?'

'Not really. The hands have been out cutting the young stuff and getting them all branded and the head counting won't be started for another few days or so, I figure. But from what Henshaw says and what I've seen, I'd say we're down a couple hundred head from what we shipped last year.'

'Could any of that be winter kill-off?'

'No. The last couple of winters have been mild. That probably means we're in for a rough one, but, oh I'd say it's been three or four years since we lost an appreciable number. Even in the worst of winters the losses are slight. Those little canyons and ravines that back up to the bluff give the herd a lot of protection.'

'But you figure there should be a few hundred head of young stuff that isn't showing up.'

'Yeah. We'll know better in a week or

so though. What are you thinking?'

'I'm not exactly sure. I stopped for a restaurant meal in town last night before coming out here and may have learned a few things. Things I'd like to check out. Anyway, I guess I'll continue keeping out of sight for another week or so. There's some more country to look at before I give up.'

Fagan noticed that Mary Ellen didn't say much, but listened attentively to what he had to say.

Turnbull sat for a moment, staring at the floor and frowning. 'You go on doing what you're doing,' he said quietly, 'meanwhile there's the rounding up of our stock to get done. We'll be about half finished with the branding soon, I reckon. When our herd is pushed across the river, I'd like you to be there. That Crown crew likes to take control of that and my hands are never able to stand up to them.'

'Well, what I've got in mind won't take but a few more days, say a week or so. I reckon I'll be back in time to help out.' Getting to his feet he hesitated a moment. 'I think I'll be taking that Crown cowboy, Collins, with me this time.'

Turnbull nodded and looking up smiled at the tall cowboy. 'You're still the ranch foreman.'

★ ★ ★

All the hired hands had left for the range by the time Fagan and the Turnbulls went into the big kitchen for their delayed breakfast. Henshaw had hung back and sat nursing a cup of coffee while Cookie served up platters of fried ham and eggs to the others. The talk around the big table focused on the condition of the range and the cattle that was being gathered at Big Flat. Henshaw agreed with what the rancher had said about the number of missing stock.

'As far as I can figure, there won't be anywhere near the herd to ship to market,' the older man said calmly.

'Winter wasn't as harsh as usual and so the losses can't be blamed on that. I figure we'll only be able to ship about half what we should have. Haven't seen what Crown's got yet, but I expect the report old Nixon has to send to the owners won't please them, either.'

Fagan smiled. 'Talking about Crown,' he said, 'I ran into that easterner while I was out riding around.' Out of the corner of his eye he saw Mary Ellen's head jerk up. Keeping his eyes down while he slowly and carefully cut a bite of ham, the cowboy continued. 'He's a strange one, that's for sure. Wanted to teach me how to box, but when he landed on his, huh, backside, decided not to bother. Wouldn't get up either. All I could do was ride away.'

'Those foreigners,' Henshaw said, trying hard not to laugh, 'can be different.' He said quietly, and then, settling his floppy Stetson squarely on his head, went outside.

★ ★ ★

Leaving them to their work, Fagan threw his saddle on a big chestnut-colored gelding and rode out after finishing breakfast. The sun was just starting to warm things up and the morning ride was pleasant. Cutting around the big barn and all the outbuildings, Fagan laughed softly as birds, flushed out of the tall grasses, flew up in bursts of colorful sound. A soft breeze bending the tops of the grass added to the gentle feeling of the morning. For some reason, he felt real good this morning.

Away from the ranch, he let the horse pick its own route, keeping the fast-moving creek on his left, holding the horse in the general direction of the bluff.

The main ranch buildings, sitting high on the lip of ravine, gave the place a clear view of the range spread out below. That view didn't include any-thing back toward the sandstone and lava bluff face sitting a mile or so behind the big log house. It was that

direction that Fagan rode this morning.
After dropping down to the creek, he'd
kneed his horse upstream. Riding along
at a comfortable trot he noticed when
the land started to climb. The creek, a
wide, slow, shallow-flowing stream
further down, soon became a narrow,
fast-moving series of cascades, the
water splashing over huge rocks and
down white-water rapids.

Reaching a flat plateau he pulled the
gelding up, letting it catch its wind. The
flat piece of land, with the creek once
again a wide meandering stream cutting
it, was almost empty of grass. Sand,
sagebrush and creosote-tarbush covered
the flats with clumps of broom
snakeweed and spindly stands of willow
growing closer to the water, Fagan saw.
The ground was mostly hardpan, the
rocks and gravels worn from the lava
flow that rose up at the far side.

Kneeing his horse forward, Fagan let
the animal pick its own path, heading
across the uneven land toward the ridge
of lava and sandstone upheaval he

could see would clearly block any further progress. Sitting high, he could see that the creek curled south before reaching the rugged, almost sheer, sandstone bluff.

'I wonder,' he asked the chestnut gelding, 'if either Turnbull or Crauley ever rode up here when they looked over their land.' The horse didn't bother answering.

'Ah ha,' he heard himself exclaim a few yards farther along, 'someone certainly has, though.' Reining the horse to a stop, he studied a stretch of bare ground. It would, he figured, take a lot of hoofed animals to make a mark on this stuff, but there it was, a clear trail running from north to south. Someone, some time, had moved a pretty good bunch of cattle across this bit of range.

'Or,' he mused, sitting with his hands folded on the saddle horn looking at dried pats of cow manure, 'someone has run a number of small jags off the range over there down to somewhere over there,' he mentally pointed first back toward the Box M's upper ranges then over toward the far side of the plateau.

'Now that would be B-Slash-B range, wouldn't it, horse? Yeah, I thought so, too. Lets go take a closer look, what do ya say?' Not getting even a flicker of an ear, he gigged the animal, reining to follow the trail.

Keeping a watch out for any movement in the distance, Fagan again let the horse set the pace. He certainly didn't want any surprises.

But that's what he got an hour's ride farther on. Pulling up suddenly, he stopped when he could see where the creek turned, disappearing into a wide-mouthed opening in the sandstone wall. The trail of hoof prints he'd been following vanished in that direction.

Someone had mentioned a trail into the badlands, he vaguely recalled. 'But didn't someone else say there was no trail across that stretch? Hmmm, wonder if that's true?'

Thinking about what it'd mean if there was a way across, he decided not to go any further. Riding blindly into something like this, he told himself, wasn't all that smart.

'That's what made the Hole-In-The-Wall such a good place for outlaws, if you'll recall,' he told the horse, reining back the way he'd come, 'hard to get in and if someone was in there didn't like you, harder to get out. No, you weren't there, were you. Well, take my word for it. This needs some thinking about. Let's go home.'

15

The ride back toward the Box M was uneventful and Fagan spent most of the time thinking about what he'd discovered. If cattle could be moved from Turnbull's range and into the badlands, then they wouldn't have to track across Crown land. Just as well, if Crown's livestock could be driven across the river south of town and then across the B-Slash-B's horse pastures, it'd be a straight shot into that opening in the bluff. That would mean working with the horse breeder.

Thinking about Crauley brought him to considering the people he'd met in the basin. Mostly they seemed to be a bunch of folks looking for their own place. A place to make a living and raise a family. Well, maybe not the blacksmith, and old Doc Adams, likely he was too old to be thinking about a family. But it certainly held true for Turnbull. Same with that pretty girl in the general store. She was wanting her own place in the world, least that's what Mary Ellen said. How about Mary Ellen? A young woman, of course she'd be thinking about her future, too, wouldn't she?

'All right, that leaves you, old son. We've had this talk before, haven't we?'

Since leaving the family ranch in West Texas he had worked a gold claim on the American River in California, rode shotgun for Wells Fargo and served as a deputy sheriff in Wyoming. His pa had argued against it when he'd first discussed leaving the Cibolo Creek Ranch, until Elias pointed out that as the youngest of four boys he'd end up working for his brothers and he wanted more than that. He wanted his own spread.

The argument was clinched when young Fagan reminded his pa that the old man himself had left the family plantation to fight in the Civil War and then join in the battle between Texas and Mexico. It was in the final days of that conflict that his pa had met the woman who was to become his mother, Adriana Christian de Salazar, the daughter of Bernardo Jose Christian Manuel de Salazar, the owner of a huge rancho that lay just south of the Rio Grande. Each of the four Fagan boys carried one of their grandfather's names.

Traveling as he did, seeing a lot of the country, it was only recently that young Fagan realized he was searching for something. What that something was he wasn't sure. Certainly it wasn't just a cattle outfit of his own. There had been a lot of opportunity for that all along the way. It wasn't danger. He'd had enough of that too. But now on the road up from Golden into the basin, for the first time he was surprised the feeling of emptiness was missing. He didn't understand it.

★ ★ ★

Back at the Box M, he found the owner and his daughter preparing for a ride into Short Creek. Henshaw was going along to help bring back the wagon of supplies needed for the remainder of the roundup.

'Mary Ellen's tired of sitting around the ranch,' Silas Turnbull laughed. 'She's peeved at me because I won't let her ride out there with the men. Darn it, Fagan, maybe you can make her see that she's no longer a wild child. She's a young woman and working with a roundup crew is no place for a woman.'

Fagan laughed. 'Mister Turnbull, if there's one person in this world that has little credit with Miss Mary Ellen, you're looking at him. All I get from her is dirty looks.'

'Yes, I've noticed that,' said Turnbull. 'Anyway, she wants to go along to visit with the Duniway girl. So, unless you've got other plans, why not ride in with us?'

★ ★ ★

On the ride into town all four kept a close eye out, remembering the attempts made by the unknown rifleman in the past, but nothing happened. There was little talk between them, with each busy with their own thoughts. In town, Turnbull left the ranch wagon and his daughter at the general store. When Fagan said something about a drink to cut the road dust, the rancher said he'd meet them a little later.

'I want to go up and visit with my lawyer friend,' Turnbull said as they walked across the street. 'I won't be long and I'll meet up with you for a drink when I'm finished.'

The saloon wasn't as empty as Fagan expected, being it wasn't Saturday and there was a roundup going on. Stepping through the swinging half-doors and letting his eyes adjust, he looked around to find a dozen or so hands in the place. Most of them sitting at the poker table toward the back or leaning against the bar. Seeing Nixon and recognizing the young gunhand, Raidler, he figured these were the tough hands Marchal had mentioned. Fagan noticed the Crauleys, both father and son, nursing drinks at the far end of the mahogany.

Finding one of the little tables near the door empty, Henshaw and Fagan pulled out chairs and, toasting each other with their drinks, settled back.

Fagan had noticed how the buzz of conversation had died out when they came into the room, but he ignored everyone and in a few minutes the soft murmur of talk took up again. Relaxing with their drinks, Henshaw was just starting to tell Fagan about how the gathering of Box M stock was going when he was interrupted by one of the Crown hands.

'Hey, there, Fagan,' the man called out. 'I hear you went and hired that fool, Sam Collins. He doing any good for ya? He should be paying his way, after all he was on Crown long enough to know what our cows look like.'

'How come is it,' Henshaw snarled, 'that every time lately a Crown man opens his mouth he's skirting around naming the Box M hands as being rustlers?' Pushing away from the table, the older man started to get to his feet. Fagan reached a hand out to stop him.

'Don't bother,' he said, and then in a louder voice he went on. 'That's what happens when the hired hands come into town in the middle of a roundup and get their noses too deep into a bottle. It frees up their mouths to loose talk.'

'Hey, Mister Big Man,' the Crown man called back, 'you got a problem with Crown men being in here for a drink? You're here. If it's all right for you and one of your men to come in it's gotta be all right for our crew, don't it?'

Fagan looked over at the man and smiled. 'Nope, it isn't any of my business what Crown's men do. I reckon if your foreman is happy with it, I haven't any complaint. However,' he went on, holding up a hand to stop the other man, 'as far as your comment about Sam, I'd have to say he is a good hand. Does his job and is earning his pay.'

Nixon's rough voice cut in. 'As long as he don't forget to keep his paws off any of our stock. It seems likely though, from what the rumor is about Turnbull running more yearlings than he's got mama cows for, that the Collins ranny'll do more than earn his forty dollars a month.'

Fagan glanced at Henshaw, shaking his head. 'Looks like our friend Nixon is making strong talk. Wonder if he can back it up?'

'Be careful, Fagan,' Henshaw warned. 'This is just like the man. He likes to start fights knowing he's never lost one. He's a killer with his fists.'

'Yeah, Mister Fagan,' Nixon's harsh voice sounded as if he had gravel in his throat, 'you better be listening to your man, there. As I recall you didn't do so good against our tenderfoot.'

The Crown hands broke out in laughter over the taunt.

'Oh, I don't know,' Fagan said slowly.

'Well, this is one time you'd better just sit back and think twice about things.'

'One of those things being the rough talk your so-called tough men are making about the spread I ride for? No, I can't hardly do that, Mister Nixon,' he let a little sneer seep into the name.

'Boy, you don't know what kind of wildcat you're messing with. If I want to repeat what I've heard, that Turnbull is rustling Crown beef, then I guess that's what I'll do. Ain't nobody around here big enough to stop me. Not unless you have to reach for that shooting iron you're packing.'

Fagan slowly pushed his beer glass to one side and pushed himself up from the table. 'All I've heard so far is you telling me how tough you are. It seems that you're looking for something to do. Maybe you've found it.'

'Yeah, just like last time. You talk big while hiding behind that six gun. Me, I do my fighting like a man, with my fists.'

Unbuckling his gun belt, Fagan smiled.

'Not in here,' Otto yelled out, slapping the top of the bar with one hand and holding a short-barreled shotgun with the other. 'Ya idiots, I told ya before, ya wanna fight, ya take it out in the street where it belongs.'

Nixon's chuckle sound like it came from deep in his chest. 'Oh, I reckon that's a good idea. That is if'n you're not turning yellow, Mister Foreman.'

Fagan made his laugh sound as relaxed and easy as he could. Fighting with someone like Nixon wasn't going to be pleasant. The man was heavily built and outweighed him by at least fifty pounds. He was also nearly twice the cowboy's age and obviously a lot more experienced. About the only thing in the Box M foreman's favor was his youth and longer arms. He had reach on Nixon but looking at the big man, and knowing there had to be something behind his brag, a fight wasn't going to be fun. He was determined not to show any lack of confidence, though.

'After you,' he smiled as he waved Nixon through the doors. Stepping to follow the big man, he noticed the young gunman, Raidler waiting to one side. A big smile split the youngster's face.

'We'll see just how big you really are, without your gun,' he sniggered.

Fagan merely shook his head and, stepping off the porch, hung his gunbelt from his saddle horn. He was turning back when Nixon came rushing in, bringing a balled fist around and into Fagan's face. Fagan ducked and the blow missed but only by a little bit, slamming like a hammer into the top of his left shoulder. The flash of pain was instantly followed by a spreading numbness as he pushed away from his horse and turned to face his attacker. The street had filled with Crown men, all lined out yelling and laughing at what they expected to see.

Fagan's shoulder slumped and his left arm hung weakly at his side.

Flexing that hand, he moved away, trying to stay away from Nixon until feeling in his shoulder returned.

'What's wrong, Mister Foreman,' someone called, 'you think you can win by running from the boss?' The crowd laughed and more calls for Nixon to do his damage were shouted out.

Nixon, letting Fagan circle, smiled. 'Oh, I don't want this to be over too quick. It's been some time since I been in a fight and I'm not in any hurry.' Quicker than Fagan expected, Nixon moved in, swinging another right fist. Fagan spun away, letting the crusty knuckles scrape the side of his head. Staggered, he sidestepped only to find Nixon right on him. Fagan felt his head explode as Nixon's fist slammed against his chin. Landing flat on his back a yard or two away, he quickly rolled, expecting Nixon to take up the attack.

'No, drifter,' the big man growled, 'it ain't gonna be that easy. First I'm gonna just knock you around a little, then when I've had enough of that, I'll show you what pain really is. C'mon, get up and let's get on with it.' Stepping back, Nixon folded his arms across his massive chest, a big smile creasing his face.

Fagan shook his head and, taking his time, slowly got to his feet. As his gaze cleared he saw Mary Ellen and her father standing to one side of the yelling cowboys. Trying to reassure her with a smile, he grimaced. His face felt like it was cracked. Putting her out of his mind and focusing on the Crown foreman he brought himself up, standing as straight as he could, sucking in a deep breath. The numbness had left his shoulder but he continued to let his arm hang down. With a final shake of his head, he brought up his right hand and, crouching a little, started circling to his right.

Nixon laughed and holding both bunched fists in front, about waist high, stepped across to block Fagan's movement. Watching Nixon's eyes, Fagan saw him squint a bit before he rushed forward, swinging both fists. Fagan instantly dropped his left shoulder, leaning away and then turned back, bringing around his left fist to smash it against Nixon's right ear.

Howling, the big man fell back, both arms coming up to protect his head. Fagan quickly stepped in, throwing one fist after another into the man's stomach just below his rib cage. Before Nixon could drop his arms, Fagan danced back, his fists up ready for another charge. Nixon stood still for a moment, glaring at his opponent.

'Ah, you're a tricky one, ain't ya. Well, that only makes it more fun. C'mon now, let's be giving the boys a show.'

With his fists out front again, Nixon lumbered straight toward Fagan, his legs steady with each step. Moving to his right, Fagan watched and when Nixon started his rush, quickly sidestepped, punching his left fist hard against the man's ear again. Nixon bawled and ducked away. Fagan pressed forward, bringing his right fist from near ground level up to connect with Nixon's nose. A bright stream of blood spurted as the man brought up his hands to cover his face. Fagan slammed fist after fist into Nixon's soft belly before stepping back out of reach. Nixon wiped a hand across his bleeding nose and, bellowing, ran at Fagan, windmilling his fists. Fagan wasn't able to duck this time and took a blow that knocked him into the dirt. Scuttling away, he got to his feet just as the foreman came rushing at him. This time Fagan stepped aside and, sticking out a booted foot, tripped the big man. Quick as a fox, Nixon hit the ground and rolled, instantly coming to his feet, fists up and ready.

The sound of the men watching the battle had receded and Fagan was no longer aware of them. His attention was directly focused on the Crown man. He'd been watching and had noticed that each time Nixon decided to throw a punch or make an attack, his eyes would narrow. Now, moving his body one way and then the other, he waited, trying to catch his breath, his fists up.

Blood still dripped from Nixon's nose and when he came in Fagan had seen the signs and was ready.

Rushing at Fagan, Nixon stretched his arms wide in an attempt to wrap the other man up in a bear hug. Fagan, hurling his fist at the middle of Nixon's face, felt his fist slide off the flattened nose and smash into an eye socket. Momentarily blinded Nixon forgot about grabbing Fagan, again his hands flying up to protect his face. Fagan, both feet planted, took advantage, swinging fist after fist as hard as he could, hammering at Nixon's lower ribs.

'Damn you,' Nixon yelled out, backhanding Fagan, knocking him away.

Again Fagan landed in the dirt of the street. This time, with one hand wiping at the blood streaming down his face, Nixon strode over and lifted a foot to stomp the downed man. Fagan, twisting away, brought his right boot up, slamming it into Nixon's crotch.

The big man's face blanched as he bent over, clutching at his groin. Fagan got to his feet. Keeping his eyes fixed on his target, he drove his fist into Nixon's exposed chin, staggering the man. Before the Crown foreman could find his balance, Fagan applied more pressure, throwing a balled fist into the soft spot just under his ribs. When Nixon bent away, clasping his middle, Fagan brought a fist crashing into the center of his face. Nixon fell over, his body rolled into a ball, arms clutching his stomach.

With legs suddenly weak and shaking, Fagan stood for a long moment looking down at the man. Around them, the Crown hands were silent.

'C'mon, boss,' Henshaw said taking Fagan's arm and leading him over to his horse. 'That's enough. He's down and that's the end of it.'

For a long minute, Fagan leaned

against his saddle, catching his breath. Slowly reaching up, he took his gun belt and was starting to buckle it around his waist when he heard Mary Ellen scream.

Whipping around, he saw Nixon, standing unsteadily on his feet, taking the Colt Raidler was handing him.

16

'Don't do it, Nixon,' Fagan yelled, grabbing his own revolver as the Crown foreman, his eyes crazed and staring fixedly, brought the weapon up.

Fagan didn't hesitate. Without a thought, he simply reacted, pulling the trigger, sending his first slug into the middle of Nixon's chest. The big man wavered and then tried again to bring his gun up. Fagan shot again, the force of the bullet turning Nixon to one side. Slowly, facing down the street, his body crumbled.

Everyone stood looking down at the dead man. Fagan stepped away from his horse.

'Raidler,' he snarled. 'You've still got one of your fancy guns. Go ahead, pull it. You want to be a big gun man, here's your chance. Go ahead,' he yelled when the young man, his face suddenly gone white, made no movement. 'Go on, you talked big and then got your boss killed. Draw it or drop it.'

Raidler didn't move. Fagan, his Colt at his side, brought it up, thumbing back the hammer. 'That's it. You either draw and I'll kill you where you stand or unbuckle and let it drop. What's it going to be?'

Quickly, his fingers trembling, Raidler let his gunbelt fall to the street.

'Listen to me, boy. You're finished around here. Get on your horse and ride. And keep riding. Because if I ever see you again, whether you're packing a gun or not, I'll think you're after me and I'll shoot you dead. Now get out of my sight before I change my mind.'

Not looking at anyone, the youngster ran across to a hitch rail and swung into a saddle. Kicking his heels against the horse's side, he thundered down the street and out of town.

★　★　★

Watching the Crown hands riding down the street, Fagan felt the tension in his body start to loosen. Dull pain throbbed where Nixon's fists had hammered him.

'That was despicable,' Mary Ellen, standing facing him, her hands planted on her hips, glared up at him. 'Brawling in the street like two overgrown boys. You could have been killed, you know. Then how could you help my father or do what you told that marshal you'd do?'

Fagan nodded. 'You're right, of course. Letting Nixon call your father a rustler was something I should have overlooked.'

'Everybody knows Father isn't a rustler.'

'Oh, it doesn't seem like that to me. But the fight's over and we can get back to the business of putting together a herd.' Stopping, he looked back down the now empty street. Turning to Henshaw, he frowned. 'Wonder what those hardcases'll do without Nixon to keep them in control. You know, I think it'd probably be a good idea to ride out and check the herd.'

'You don't think they'll do anything, do you?' asked Mary Ellen, worry lines filling her forehead.

'Maybe, and then again, maybe not. It won't hurt to be there if they are thinking about causing trouble, though.'

Henshaw handed Fagan the reins of the chestnut, 'C'mon, boss. It didn't look like they was in any hurry. Maybe we can get there to help out if they do decide to do anything.'

Fagan nodded and swinging into the saddle, gave the woman as much of a smile as his sore face would allow. 'Guess you'll have to collect your pa and find your own way home. Don't bother telling Miss Abigail hello for me.'

Riding alongside Henshaw as they kicked their horses into a gallop down the street and out of town, he didn't see George Crauley standing on the porch watching.

'Damn it all, that ain't good news for us, Nixon getting hisself killed like that.' Crauley cursed under his breath.

'What the hell do we care, Pa. That Nixon never did like us much anyhow. I say it's a good thing, seeing him laying there in the dirt.'

'Boy, you ain't got the brains God gave a goose. Without the stock Nixon and his men been stealing and running over to our place, there ain't any way we can go on sending herds over the trail. We'll be back to picking up a handful here or there and I kinda like having a bigger herd to sell. He was our cover, long as we was sending cattle over to that crooked buyer we was making real money. That damn fool thought we was working for Nixon. No, without Nixon's mark on the bill of sale, we're out of business. With him dead, we're done.'

'There's still that last bunch Nixon's men ran over. We got them back in that little valley. We can always run them over to the loading pens and go set up somewheres else, can't we?'

'Dammit, boy, I don't want to set up somewhere else. I like it right fine here, with our own spread.'

'Well, then, what'll we do?'

'I dunno. We haven't sold enough stock all year to keep the ranch going. We gotta have the money we made from running Crown and Box M beef down the trail. Let's get back to the ranch. I gotta think what to do. Get the horses and meet me around back.'

★ ★ ★

With Henshaw at his side Fagan rode out of town and, instead of taking the wagon road back to the Box M, cut across country toward Big Flats. Keeping the horses at a steady pace, he figured they would be reaching the Big Flat holding ground at about the same time as the Crown riders would get there. If, that is, Nixon's tough men were heading that way.

Of course, there would be the rest of

Box M's hands already there, finishing up the cutting and branding. Mostly those were punchers, some of them family men, not hard gunmen. Whether they would stand up to Nixon's toughs or not would remain to be seen.

Henshaw didn't say anything, but wondered how Fagan was going to hold up. It'd been a good day's work, as far as he could see, first beating Nixon and then killing the big man. The rustling of stock from the basin had always seemed not to bother Nixon as much as you'd think. Talking about it with Moses, they had reasoned that the Crown foreman had been stealing stock from the New York owner for some time but could not figure out how to prove it. Then when Caldwell's body had been found, they didn't know what could be done. Now with Nixon dead, maybe it'd jar something loose. He had to hand it to the young stranger; he half smiled to himself, this Fagan had been busy.

Their horses were breathing heavily

when they reached the first sign of the herd.

'Hey, you're just in time,' Moses called as they rode up to the chuck wagon. Most of the hands were standing with tin plates, waiting for Cookie to start ladling out the grub. 'There's a big pot of stew. Of course, you'll have to put in yore time afterwards with the working class to pay for it.' He chuckled, pointing out where a few mounted men could be seen riding slowly around the bunched up herd. 'We'll be ready to start moving the herd across the river tomorrow, I figure.'

Nodding at the cook, Fagan took two cups from the stack and filled them from the huge fire-blackened pot that was sitting on a flat rock next to the cook fire. Handing one to Henshaw, he held up a hand to stop the crew's laughter.

'Boys, we maybe have a problem. First thing is to let you know that Nixon is dead.' The laughter had stopped, and at his words silence halted the teasing comments.

'Just so you get it right, let me explain that he and I had a fight. And,' Fagan raised his voice over the barrage of questions, 'at the end of it, Nixon was handed a six-gun and, well, I shot him.'

Nobody said anything. Henshaw nodded. 'It was all fair. There'd been some talk and one thing led to another. Nixon thought he'd run roughshod over Fagan here, but didn't. You know how he was, a bully. Well, just like you heard, he took his beating and then made a play for a gun and lost.'

'What'll that mean to us out here?' one of the hands called.

Fagan shook his head. 'I don't know. I suppose the roundup will have to continue and a combined herd'll still have to be driven down to the railhead at Golden. That'll have to be done no matter who's running things over at Crown. But what's more important right now is what we think is likely.

That gang of thugs that Nixon had on the payroll were in town with him and they left right after Nixon went down. I got a feeling they'll be coming here pretty quick.'

'What do ya mean? Why'd they come out here. They've got nothing to do with the gather, do they?' someone asked.

Sam Collins took a hesitant step forward. 'Boys, I think Mr Fagan's right. Those fellas weren't part of the crews and now, all of a sudden they're out of a job. It was never clear why Nixon kept them around, but he did. And there was always talk about some rustling going on. Now I ain't saying nothing or accusing anyone of anything, but if those old boys think they've got money coming where do you think they'll come calling to collect it? Not back to the ranch, I'd say. Mister Peeters wouldn't pay them anything. I happened to know he didn't like having them around.'

Henshaw leaned over to Fagan and

whispered. 'I wondered what it'd take to get that man talking. He's done a good job since you hired him. He's a good man and most everyone likes him. They'll listen to him.'

'Well, whatever you decide,' another man yelled, 'ya better do it quick. Looky over there and you'll see a bunch of riders heading this way.'

Fagan and Henshaw had beaten them to the herd, but not by much.

17

'Hold up there, boys,' Fagan called out when the bunch of riders got close enough. Sitting slouched in the saddle and holding up his left hand, his right holding a saddle gun which was pointed at the sky, the rifle stock resting on his thigh, he made his intentions clear. Seeing the Box M hands standing in a ragged line behind the foreman, the tough-looking bunch pulled up. For a long moment the riders sat on their milling horses, waiting for someone to give an order.

'Now, whatever you're looking for just isn't here,' Fagan said loud enough to be heard before any of Nixon's gang could make a decision. 'This herd's all carrying the Box M brand, Crown is over across the river, that way.' He used the rifle barrel to point, letting it drop so it was pointing directly at one of the riders.

Without a leader and considering the number of rifles and belt-guns facing them, the man Fagan had in his sights reined around and without a word, jabbed spurs into his mount's side. As quick as they had ridden up the bunch turned to ride away.

'Whew,' Collins said, glancing over his shoulder at the other hands. 'Now I, for one, didn't like that at all. What I wouldn't give for a drink of rotgut right about now.'

Laughing at his comment, the tension that had filled the cowboys quickly disappeared.

'All right, boys,' Henshaw called out, 'let's finish our afternoon coffee and get back to making up a herd.'

When the hands turned away to follow the order, Henshaw turned to Fagan. 'Do ya think that'll be the end of it? Think they'll leave us alone, now?'

'I don't know. With Crown's foreman dead, I reckon someone will have to go talk with whoever's going to be running the show over there. That should be Mr Turnbull. Guess that's my next stop. I think I'd like to take Collins with me if you don't mind. There's another thing or two I want to check on and I'd like someone backing me up.'

'Take him and do what you gotta do. I'll keep this end of things going. Let us know what's what. I figure we'll be ready to start moving them in about a few more days.'

★ ★ ★

Fagan made it clear to Collins that riding with him might mean riding into some danger.

'Better stop by the ranch and pick up a box of shells for that rifle of yours,' said the foreman after Collins agreed to ride shotgun. Collins only nodded and swung into the saddle.

It was late afternoon when Fagan and Collins rode into the ranch yard. Hoping not to be seen riding across the upper sections of Crauley's range, they decided to wait for morning before riding out.

Talking with Turnbull about the men turning Nixon's tough men away, the older man agreed that someone would have to go talk with Peeters. When Fagan mentioned his plan to take Collins for a little ride in the morning, the rancher nodded and said he'd ride over to Crown's headquarters.

Both Fagan and Collins were out of their bunks and saddling up at first light. This time Fagan had roped a three-year-old bay. Collins dropped his loop over the head of a brown and white pinto. Hoping to have the opportunity to talk with Mary Ellen, Fagan took his time over a last cup of coffee but felt he could push it only so far. With the sun peaking over the black horizon of the mountains far across the basin to the east, the two rode up back of the ranch buildings, following the route Fagan had ridden before.

Taking a more direct route to the opening they rode up to the wide entrance a couple hours later. Sitting their saddles, the two men studied the wide entrance into the water-washed defile while giving their horses a breather and a drink from the creek flowing out of the mouth of what appeared to be a gap leading back into the sandstone bluff.

'Looks to me like there's been a lot more stock run in there than what's come from the Box M side of the range,' said Sam Collins, pointing with a wave of his hand to a heavily churned up stretch of soft sand.

When he'd first found the mouth of this fissure, Fagan hadn't ridden far enough to see the ground the cowhand was looking at. He'd been following the sign coming from his home ranch. Looking over to what Collins was talking about, he saw sign that a large number of hoofed animals had been driven into this break. Hard to tell exactly when, but he didn't think it'd been long ago.

'These are cow prints,' Collins

murmured, 'and if I recall, the Crauleys are horse breeders. Wonder just whose cattle came this way?'

'They'd have to be from Crown. Makes it look like horses aren't the only livestock those Crauleys are interested in. From what I was told, the B-slash-B buildings are back that way a mile or so from the bluffs. It'd be mighty hard to miss being that close to this many moving cattle and not know it.'

'Yep. You know, there's been a time or two in town when I've seen George Senior sharing a drink with Nixon. Always standing off at the end of the bar by themselves, heads together like they was planning the overthrow of the government or something.'

Fagan nodded. 'Alright, here's how we'll handle it. You backtrack this trail and I'll ride on in to see where they were taken. Ride slow and keep out of sight. All I want to do now is find out what's going on. It's still early in the day so let's plan on meeting back here around noontime. If you get here ahead of me, find yourself a bit of shade,' he waved a hand toward the shadowed draw, 'and wait. I'll be along.'

'What exactly are you looking for, boss? Seems to me that, as foreman, your job would be over at the gather. I noticed even after your fake death you didn't show up out at Big Flats much. Care to let me in on it?'

'Well, yeah, you're right. I was asked by the law down in Golden to see what I could find out about reports of cattle being rustled up here. Mr Turnbull had telegraphed the marshal down there and, seeing as I was coming this way, he asked me to take a look. Now, as I mentioned before, there could be some danger involved with this. Someone shot Turnbull's last foreman, Caldwell, remember, and there's those shots taken at me. If you want, you can go on back to the Big Flats and no hard feelings.'

'Not likely,' Collins laughed. 'Chasing after a bunch of squalling beef gets old real quick. No, sir, I'll go along and see if I can find out where these critters come from. Meet you up in the shade in a couple hours.' Reining away, he rode off without looking back.

Fagan sat looking into the opening. Sitting in the bright morning sun, all he could see was darkening shadows with the creek flowing down the center of the steep-sided canyon walls. Kneeing the bay, and keeping to the middle of the creek, he rode into darkness.

Once his eyes adjusted to the gloom he could see how the rough mixture of black lava rock and gritty brown sandstone opened into a corridor that wandered in a series of long winding curves. High overhead the clear blue sky appeared to be brighter. Probably, he figured, because he was seeing it from the dimness of the shade.

Riding at a slow walk, he was surprised to see little narrow side canyons open up along the way. Small streams of water flowed out of some of these, joining the creek.

Without seeing the sun it was hard to

judge how long he'd been riding when he suddenly came out into full sunshine. Reining back, he sat looking out over a long narrow valley encircled by the high sandstone walls. The creek followed the near wall pouring out of the green scum of a pond. Cattle, moving about as they grazed, covered the valley floor. Taking it all in, Fagan spotted a thin stream of gray-white smoke rising from the tin stove pipe sticking through the roof of a rundown, ramshackle log cabin on the other side of the pond.

'Looks inviting, don't it?' The question, along with the sound of a gun being cocked, come from somewhere behind him.

18

'That's good, just sit nice and still,' the man's voice went on. 'Don't go reaching for your shooting iron. Fact is, it'd probably be good of you to unbuckle that gun-belt and reach it back to me. The same with your rifle, too.'

Whoever it was, Fagan figured, he was a little above him. If the man had a rifle it wouldn't pay to not do as he was told. Shucking his hardware, he shook his head at not being more cautious.

'Guess riding in to explore wasn't such a good idea,' he called back over a shoulder. 'Always wondered what was back here. Now I know. There's no reason for you to get antsy, though. I'm just a wandering cowhand.'

The unseen man chuckled. 'Now that was a good try, Mister Fagan. But it won't work. I know who you are.

Enough talk. Just head on over toward the cabin. And do it carefully. I'm pretty good with this long gun if I say so myself.'

The cabin was a couple hundred feet from the pond, which Fagan saw now was mostly shallow swampy marsh, with stands of willows and other brush lining its banks except where cattle had come in for water. Riding up to the structure he sat his saddle and waited.

'Just climb down, Mister Fagan and keep both your hands on the horn. I'll be watching.'

With a rifle poking him in the back, Fagan pushed through the door. Typical of line shacks on every ranch, rope-bottomed bunk beds lined two walls, a sheet metal stove stood close to another. A rickety table and a few chairs were the only furniture. Told to take one of the rawhide-bottomed chairs and put his hands behind his back, his wrists were quickly tied, likely with thin leather pigging strings, the kind every cowboy carried.

'You're dead meat, old son,' his captor stepped around and stood smiling down at him. He was a big man, tall and lanky. His whiskery face looked hard and wind burned. It was a face, Fagan thought, he had seen before but couldn't think of where or when.

'Naw, we never met,' he said, hooking a chair with a toe and sitting down. 'But I know you. Saw you when you was carrying a badge up in Jackson County. I'd come down from the Hole-In-The-Wall a short time after you and those town folks shot up Ketchum and his boys. Name's Russell. They call me Long Tom Russell.'

'Guess I never heard of you,' Fagan let a smile pass his lips. Keeping his movement hidden, he started working on the pigging strings.

'No reason for you to. Black Jack hadn't neither. I wanted to go along with him to hit that bank but he didn't know me. Said he had enough men and didn't need me. Well, look what that got him.'

'You're the second fella I've met that's claimed to have been part of the Hole-In-The-Wall gang. How many more or you are there hanging around these parts?'

Russell laughed. 'You mean that fool kid, Raidler? Hells fire, he wasn't nothing. You shoulda shot him when you had him under the gun.'

'Well, maybe. Tell me, how come you didn't just drop me? Are you the one that's tried and missed those times?'

'Nope. I wouldn't have missed, it been me. Naw, that was George Crauley's boy. He was quite proud of hisself, until you came marching into the saloon all healthy and happy. No sir. Now look at ya, all tied up like a Christmas goose just awaiting for the oven,' Russell chuckled and leaned back in his chair.

'Don't think I don't appreciate it, but why am I still alive? Coming into this valley and finding those beeves out there, well, there's no way you can let me ride out. So, what stopped you from simply shooting me?' Fagan continued working on the leather pigging string that bound his wrists to the back of the chair. Every cowboy used a pigging string the same way, a half-hitch around a calf's rear leg, then a couple quick turns around one or more front legs finishing off with another half-hitch. Even when being branded, the animal strained against that long strip of leather, kept the hitches tight. Fagan worked at keeping the pressure off.

'Oh, didn't I tell you? That's the oven I was talking about. It's that Crauley kid, George Junior. Old George made a big thing about it, back when the kid caught the foreman of the Box M ranch out there snooping around. Yeah, Crauley thought his kid was finally growing up. Then when Junior got back from Golden, all puffed up and proud, the old man almost bought everyone a cigar. Ha! But then you came riding in. You think the old man didn't let him have it after the boy had just got through bragging about how he'd shot you outa the saddle? Now the order is that we get the chance, we hold you so little Junior has another crack at ya.' This struck Russell as being funny and he reared back with more laughter.

'You know,' Fagan, not seeing the joke, hadn't laughed, 'there's a lot going on here I just don't get. Why would the Crauleys care about killing me? Hells bells, all I am is a cowpuncher working for the smallest spread in the basin.'

'Nope, don't do ya any good trying that one me either. The word is that you're working for that marshal down in Golden.'

Fagan shook his head, looking up at the pole rafters. For a little time he thought he'd felt a small loosening in the pigging string. 'Well,' he said, hoping to keep the other man's attention elsewhere, 'I guess it won't do any good to say that's hogwash.'

'Don't matter none to me. Junior said he saw you meeting with the lawman down there and that's enough.'

'So Junior is part of the rustling

that's going on here in the basin?'

'Part of it, hell's fire, old son, he and his pa is all of it. Don't you know nothing?'

'Nope. Like I said, I'm just a cowhand.' Fagan stopped moving his fingers a minute, then, putting what he hoped was a questioning look on his face, went on. 'Everybody tells me that the foreman over at Crown had been stealing his boss's beef. Others think it's a wild bunch from back in these badlands that've been doing the rustling. Now you say it's the Crauleys. Too much for me to understand.'

'Well, it don't matter none I guess, so I'll tell you . . . all those folk are right. Nixon has been running off Crown cattle since he went to work there. Of course, we've been giving him a little help along the way. But it's old George Crauley that's leading the pack. You just can't see it, can you?' he said dismissively. 'Me'n a few of the boys came down here looking for beef we could run up north into the mining

238

camps. George and his boy and me and a couple others. George knew Nixon from some place, maybe over in California. I kinda overheard them talking one time. Anyway when they run into each other here they put their heads together and worked it out. Nixon and his hardcases would move a few head close to the river and let George know where they'd be. We'd go get 'em. Run them here and when we got a sizable herd, drive them on out to a rail siding over on the other side of the badlands. We'd have a receipt signed by the Crown foreman to give to the buyer and everyone was happy.'

'You're saying Crauley's horse breeding operation is phony?'

'Naw. It started out to be but then he found out he could make money swapping off horses to men on the owl hoot trail, working the brands a bit or make up new sales paper, sending them on down south or back east. No, the B-slash-B is a real enough ranch, all right. He even went down and registered the brand so it'd look all nice and legal. You'd be surprised how many horses we use up, chasing a herd through the badlands and out to the railhead. Old George even has plans on making this here little valley another Hole-In-The-Wall. Fellas riding the back trails could come in here and for a price have a place to hide out. They could get their grub from Crauley and, when they rode out, be on a fresh horse. Oh, he had plans, he did. You shooting Nixon killed that idea, though.'

Finally Fagan felt slack in the pigging string. 'Why? He doesn't need Nixon, does he?'

'Well, yeah. I figure the horse breeding operation isn't enough for him. He's gotta have the money from selling Crown beef. It's an almost steady stream of livestock that could be run through here. Crown's so big, if nobody got greedy they could take the cream off the crop for years. Add a handful from the Box M only makes it better. But without that foreman's signed bill of sale, his buyer won't deal with him. That's what's happening right now,' Russell's smile indicated self-satisfaction. 'While you're sitting here, he's got those toughs Nixon hired to go get the roundup herd and start it moving in this direction. It'll be one last drive, the best from the Box M and from Crown, along with the couple hundred head that's already here. Nobody is going to figure out where to look for that herd, at least not until we're long gone. Everyone'll be looking south, trying to find where they went.'

'And from here they'll be moved on through the badlands, over to a railhead on west of here?'

'Yep. There's a trail clear across to the other side. And over there is a narrow gauge rail line. It's a little feeder line from farther up north, hooking up with the Denver and Union Pacific line at Golden. That buyer Crauley knows ships all kinds of equipment and freight up into the gold fields. On the way north he has a string of cattle cars dropped off at a little siding. We load them cars up and the train picks them up on their way back south. From there it's a straight shot back east to the slaughter house. No questions asked.'

With his wrists loose, Fagan held tight to the pigging string to keep it from dropping to the rough plank floor. Now all he had to do was choose the right time.

★ ★ ★

That moment came when Russell, placing both hands on the table to push himself up, started to get out of the chair. In one smooth movement, Fagan, holding on to the back of his chair stood up bringing the chair around, smashing it into the man's surprised face, knocking him to the floor.

Quickly stripping the Colt from Russell's holster, Fagan stood back.

'Now, it's your turn to be nice and still.'

Using a boot, he jabbed the outlaw in the side. 'Roll on over and put your hands behind you.'

Using the same pigging string, but being careful to tie better knots, he secured Russell's wrists. Tearing a strip off a worn sheet taken from one of the bunk beds, he wrapped the man's ankles together.

'Here's what I would suggest, Russell,' said Fagan, sitting back in one of the chairs. 'Sooner or later you'll figure out how to get loose. Now whatever you do then is up to you, but if it was me I wouldn't hang around here long. Crauley's plan to high-grade that roundup herd is going to fall flat. Any idea of using this little valley as a hideout is not good thinking, either. Think about it. The famous Hole-In-The-Wall didn't last much longer than the gang that used it. Do what you want, but don't show up in Short Creek or I might think you're coming for me.

It didn't work for Nixon; it won't work for you. I'd go the other way, was I you. Maybe Oregon or even California.'

Strapping his own gun belt around his waist, he tossed Russell's pistol and rifle out toward the middle of the pond.

'C'mon horse,' he said swinging into the saddle, 'you've had all afternoon to rest. Let's go cause someone some trouble.'

19

Collins had no more than ridden into the shadows when Fagan came riding down the middle of the creek.

'Well, now. I was hoping I'd get to set back and have a smoke while waiting for you,' he groused, reining in. 'What'd you find back in there?'

Letting the bay drink, Fagan told him about the valley and the trail across to the other side.

'I happened to meet up with one of the crowd that has been running off with Crown and Box M stock. He mentioned a rail siding on the far side of this so-called badlands.'

Collins frowned. 'You run into one of the rustlers? And he's still back there?'

'Yeah. Well, he was when I left him. I got a feeling he'll be long gone by now, though. He also explained how those men that were riding with Nixon are planning on taking the roundup herd and bringing them this way. My thought is for us to go back to the Box M and warn Turnbull. If he and the crew are ready, Nixon's gang can be stopped. They were about ready to start their herd across to join up with Crown's so if we hurry we should be able to catch up with them somewhere along the line.'

'Well, I backtracked that trail and it does slip past Crauley's horse pastures. I figure it crosses the river just below town a mile or so. There's a wide shallow ford that's seen a lot of traffic. You gotta look close, but the sign is there. That'd be the quickest way from here on to Crown land.'

'That's something else we'll have to deal with. It seems Crauley is behind all the rustling. He can be taken care of after we stop Nixon's gang.'

'Crauley? Mixed up with Nixon? Boy, that don't leave many honest ranchers in the basin, does it?' Seeing Fagan's frown, Collins quickly went on. 'OK, I guess old man Turnbull's one of them.'

'C'mon. Let's ride.'

* * *

It was late in the day when Fagan and Collins rode into the Box M yard. Not stopping at the ranch house, they headed directly to the big corral and stripped the saddles from their horses and gave them a rubdown. Roping fresh mounts, they were cinching up their saddles when Mary Ellen came running from the big house.

'Elias, I'm glad I caught you. Dad's gone out to the herd. He wanted to help out making the drive across to join up with the Crown herd. I tried to talk him out of it, but he's just too darn stubborn. Are you two heading out there now?'

'We're on our way,' Fagan didn't think it would do any good to say any more than that.

'Saddle my horse and I'll go with you,' she called, turning to run back

247

toward the house.

'That's not a good idea, miss,' Fagan called. 'You're better off staying here. We'll head on out and talk your pa into coming back in. It'll be dark before we get there and, well, that's no place for a young lady.'

Not waiting for her argument, he nodded at Collins and swung into the saddle. The two left the yard at a gallop.

'Damn,' Fagan cursed when he saw the herd had already been pushed off the Big Flats holding grounds. It was well past dusk but there was still enough light to see that the prairie around the big pond was empty. The herd had been moved already. 'I was afraid of that. Henshaw said they'd be ready to start moving the herd but I was hoping . . . ah, well. No reason for us to go banging around in the dark. Let's hunker down here and get an early start in the morning.'

Neither man had thought to bring more than the sandwiches they'd packed before riding out that morning so the night camp was a hungry one. Both were up and had their bedrolls tied behind their saddles at first light.

Crossing the river it was easy to follow the churned-up path left by the Box M herd. The sun was just clearing the far horizon when they heard the snap of gunshots coming from somewhere ahead of them.

'Those damn fools are getting a little anxious,' Collins yelled. 'They're trying to take over the herd.'

'Let's see what we can do,' Fagan called, jabbing his spurs into his horse's sides and pulling his Winchester free.

Topping a low rise, they could see that the Box M herd had joined up with Crown's. The combined herd was one big mass where they had been bedded down. Almost as one, as panic started by the gunfire, the animals were gaining their feet. Fagan had seen it happen before, that panic would grow and there would be a stampede.

Coming from the side of the herd closest to the river, Fagan saw a dozen

249

or so riders heading toward where two chuck wagons stood. Around the wagons, men, quickly pulling on their pants and grabbing weapons were rushing to meet that charge. The cattle, in full fright, rushed to get away from the sharp noise. The stampede moved away, leaving the chuck wagons and galloping riders behind in a cloud of thick dust.

'C'mon,' Fagan yelled, 'they won't expect help coming from this direction.'

His horse, feeling the excitement, needed no urging but in a bound was running full out. Draping the reins over the saddle horn, Fagan used both hands, bringing the rifle up and without taking time to aim, squeezing the trigger. Levering and firing as quickly as he could, he saw the rustlers' charge begin to break up. Faintly, as if from far away, he heard Collins, bellowing a rebel yell and shooting.

Rushing into the haze of dust, Fagan felt his horse stumble. Instinctively kicking free of the stirrups, he threw himself off as the big animal crumbled, landing in a heap.

For a long moment, Fagan lay stunned, trying to catch his breath. Slowly sitting up he looked around, trying to see what had happened. A few feet away, a man's body lay all curled up on its side. Still too shaky to stand, he crawled to the man and turned him on his back. The man's hand still holding a Colt six-gun flopped against Fagan's leg. The front of the man's shirt was covered in dirt-smeared blood. His face had been rubbed raw against the ground but it was still recognizable. Fagan could only shake his head. The dead man was George Crauley.

'Well, will you looky here,' someone snarled above him.

Wiping the dirt from his face, Fagan, his vision still unsettled, turned to see who had snuck up on him. Slowly, as his sight cleared, he knew he was in trouble. George Junior, leaning forward in his saddle, his rifle pointed directly at Fagan's head.

'Who's that there,' young Crauly snarled, 'one of your hired hands?'

Fagan just shook his head, never taking his eyes off that rifle barrel.

'Hey,' Junior bellowed, finally seeing who the dead man was, 'that's Pa. You've killed my pa, you ... damn you,' his face went white. Raising the rifle to his shoulder, eyes black with hatred, his finger tightened on the trigger. 'I'd say your luck has finally left you. Twice I missed you, but it don't look like it'll happen again. That stampede was a good idea of Pa's. Well, a piss poor idea it was, too. Scatter the hired help, he said, and run the cattle a mite. We can round up enough later to make it pay. But look what happened. He's dead. But yore here. Kinda like an extra bonus I get. Mister Fagan, the famous killer of outlaws, just lying there in the dirt. Ha!'

Fagan, caught kneeling by the dead man's body, didn't need to look to know he'd never be able to pull his Colt in time. All the boy had to do was touch the trigger and he was dead. Trying to see a way out of it, he could only watch as Junior's finger twitched.

At the instant the rifle fired, Junior's horse took a step forward and the shot went over Fagan's shoulder. Not thinking, Fagan reached down and grabbed the pistol from the dead man's hand. Bringing it up, he didn't hesitate. Without stopping his motion, he thumbed back the hammer, sending the bullet square into Junior's chest.

Junior, knocked backward, slid off the horse's rump landing flat on his back. Keeping the pistol ready, Fagan got to his feet and moving unsteadily, stepped over to look down at the wounded man. Blood poured from a hole in young man's shirt.

'Pa,' Junior called, his eyes flashing wildly one way and then the other. 'Pa, help me, Pa.' Fagan watched as he stopped moving. Softly, as if from far away, Junior called out once more, 'Pa.' And died.

Dropping Crauley's Colt, Fagan

walked back, looking for his rifle. Wiping the dust and dirt from it he made his way toward the chuck wagons. Through the dust fog he saw other men standing around, dazed at what had happened.

One of the first he recognized, dirt streaks lining his face, was Henshaw. The older man didn't look happy.

'Hey, there, Mister Fagan. Glad to see you got here in time to worry that gang of fools.'

'Yeah. Any sign of Collins?'

'Yeah, he's all right. As far as I know, we lost five men, three from Crown's crew and two of ours.' Letting his gaze fall, his voice wavered a little, 'one of those is Mr Turnbull.'

'Ah, no. Was he shot?'

'No. Got caught in the stampede. Looks like he tried to get ahead of them and turn the leaders. Damn fool thing to do.'

20

Fagan borrowed a ranch wagon from Crown to bring the Box M's bodies back to the ranch. He had wrapped Silas Turnbull's body in a blanket and wouldn't let Mary Ellen unwrap it. She cried and fought him, but once he told her how her father had died, understood. All the men were buried on a hill overlooking the ranch house.

'Ma's buried there,' Mary Ellen had explained.

Most of the crew had stayed back at Crown, working to gather the market herd. A few hands were sent into the badlands to bring out the cattle hidden away there. After the funeral, Henshaw had ridden back to help out and Fagan had stayed at the ranch.

'What will you do now?' Mary Ellen asked him at breakfast the next morning. 'I know you were only going to stay until after the roundup. You've stopped the rustling that's been going on, but, well, I'm going to need some help and,' her words suddenly came in a rush, 'I'd like you to stay.'

Looking up at her, Fagan smiled. 'I've drifted all around the country, looking for something but not knowing exactly what. Somehow I think this may have been it. Yeah, I'd like to stay on.'

For the first time since learning of her father's death, Mary Ellen smiled.

★ ★ ★

Riding over to Crown later in the day, Fagan was surprised to find the eastern dude, Peeters, sitting at the chuck wagon.

'I've hired a new foreman,' he said by way of greeting Fagan. 'A couple of the men suggested that I ask one of your hands to take the job. I do trust you don't mind.'

'And he agreed? Who is it?' Fagan

hoped it wouldn't be Henshaw.

'Sam Collins. The men assured me he was the best one for the position.'

Feeling relief, Fagan could only nod.

'He tells me the herd is about ready,' Peeters went on, 'to start the drive. The men have done a headcount and it appears that only a few head were lost. Will you travel with the herd?'

'No. I agree with what you've been told. Collins is a good man. Let him make the drive.'

★   ★   ★

Fagan, Henshaw and most of the Box M crew returned to the home ranch and things had started to return to normal when one afternoon a man came riding out carrying a letter from town for Mary Ellen.

'Elias,' she called to Fagan after reading the note, 'that lawyer, Mr Lukas, would like us to come in and talk with him. I've wanted to ride in. Can we do it in the morning?'

That ride in was more enjoyable than usual. This time Fagan sat next to Mary Ellen and handled the reins while Henshaw followed along behind. Neither of the two heard the older man's chuckle at times.

The visit to the lawyer's office was quick.

'Miss Turnbull, Mr Fagan,' the lawyer, a thin man, greeted the pair, smiling at Mary Ellen and thrusting a boney hand out to Fagan. 'Thank you for taking the time to come in. What I have to discuss with you is your father's will, Miss Turnbull.'

'I didn't know he had one.'

'Yes. He came in a few weeks ago and I helped him make it out.' Glancing at Fagan, he let a dry little smile play on his thin lips. 'Your father was worried, you see. If something should happen to him, he explained, he wanted to make sure you were taken care of. His idea was to leave half the Box M ranch to Mr Fagan.'

'What?' It had caught Fagan off guard.

'Yes. Of course, there is one provision to that. You see,' Lukas dropped his eyes to the papers he held, his face turning pink with embarrassment, 'according to what Mister Turnbull told me, he'd noticed how you look at his daughter and he thought he knew her well enough to know how she felt. So, if you, Mr Fagan, agree to stay on at the Box M and help Miss Mary Ellen, then you become half owner. However, if you decide to ride on, then the entire ranch remains in Miss Mary Ellen's ownership.'

'We've already discussed this,' said Mary Ellen calmly before Fagan could speak. 'Elias has agreed to stay on, so that's that.'

Back on the street, with Fagan still not sure how to think about what had happened, Mary Ellen took his arm and pointed.

'There's Abigail and that Mr Peeters. I want to go talk with her.'

'Uh huh,' Fagan nodded. 'I think I have a few things to talk over with that Mr Peeters, myself.'

'Now, Elias, you're not going to cause trouble for her, are you? She's my best friend and, well, just don't go causing trouble.'

'Nope, if anything, it's just the opposite.'

After saying their hello's, the two women walked on toward the general store, leaving the men standing alone.

'Peeters, let's go have a drink. I've got something to talk to you about.'

In the saloon, the two men took their drinks over to a table against the wall and, after sitting down were quiet for a moment, relaxed in the soft gloom of the long narrow room.

'Now as I recall,' Fagan said after a bit, 'you said something about wanting to go back home, to New York. Are you still thinking that way?'

'Oh, yes. I'm not cut out for this kind of life. There's too much emptiness, if you see what I mean. Look out there on the street. There is hardly anyone doing anything. Except for over at Abigail's store, there is not really any business going on. That's where I'm most comfortable, where things are happening.'

'But you can't leave until your father says you can? Is that it?'

Wearily Peeters nodded. 'He thinks I need to get toughened up. I'm not exactly sure what he means by that and I doubt if he does. I don't know,' he sighed.

'Well, then. What if he got a report that the man who has been his ranch foreman for a number of years had been stealing him blind? However, you let him know that thing has been worked out and that the rustling of Crown livestock has been stopped. Not only that, you can give assurances that the thief has been punished. Do you think, if your description was worded right, your father would think you had done a good job and had learned by it?'

'But I didn't have anything to do

with Nixon getting caught. You did all that.'

'Uh huh. Maybe. But your pa doesn't have to know that, does he?' Holding up a hand to stop from being interrupted, Fagan quickly went on. 'You wouldn't have to tell a lie, exactly. Just write him your account, leaving out my name and not putting in yours. If you're as smart a businessman as you think you are, then that shouldn't be hard.'

Sipping his drink, Peeters thought about it. Finally, letting a smile start to grow, he nodded. 'It might work.'

'And if it did,' Fagan added softly, 'would you ask Miss Abigail to go back with you?'

'Oh, most definitely. Yes, I'd ask for her hand in matrimony in an instant.'

'Good for you, old son. Good for you. Now, finish up your drink and go start writing to your pa. I've got to go send a telegram to the marshal down in Golden telling him to have a talk with a certain cattle buyer.'

'Oh, I do hope Winston's father lets him come back home soon,' Abigail Duniway sighed, talking with Mary Ellen. 'You're getting what you want. It's almost not fair.'

The two women were standing at the counter of the general store, not paying any attention to Henshaw who was slowly going through a pile of work shirts.

'Oh, Abby, I miss my father but I'm so glad he made Elias half-owner in the ranch. I was afraid he'd think Elias, well, wasn't good enough. I mean just being a drifting cowpoke and all. You know how men can be at times.'

'Yes. That will make it nice for you. Winston doesn't have to worry about things like that. I mean, well, you know what I mean.'

'Yes,' Mary Ellen sighed.

'Miss,' said Henshaw stepping around the table and walking over to the counter. 'I reckon there's something you should know about that man of yours, Fagan.'

'Oh, Henshaw,' Mary Ellen cried, her forehead furrowed in a frown, 'Don't you dare tell me something bad about him. I just won't listen.'

'No ma'am, just the opposite. You see, you all think Elias Fagan is just a drifter. Wal, I gotta tell you, his pa is Alexanda Sebastian Fagan, owner of the Cibolo Creek Ranch down in south Texas. Either of you ever hear of that spread?'

'No, I haven't,' Mary Ellen said. Abigail shook her head but didn't say anything.

'Wal, let me tell you. The Cibolo Creek Ranch is on the Texas-Mexican border and covers nearly a hundred thousand acres on the US side with title to another fifty thousand acres or so across the river.' Chuckling he went on, 'that means that your Mr Fagan is heir to a ranch as big if not bigger than Crown. Now, does that sound like a drifter?'

Both young women stood speechless.

'Why . . . but — ' Mary Ellen tried to gather her thoughts.

Abigail smiled a little and then, almost as if talking to herself, said softly, 'Bigger than Crown?'

Hearing her friend, Mary Ellen glanced over, catching the look in Abigail's eye.

'Don't even think about it,' she warned her voice hard and unrelenting. 'Mr Fagan is part owner of the Box M and he's mine. Maybe it's time you started packing for a trip back east.'

Henshaw, quietly stepping aside, kept his laughter to himself.

THE END